Granger protecte flames. "Hold on,

He went behind the SUV and brought the butt of his weapon up. He rammed the metal against the glass. Then again. The glass was stronger here. Pain cut through him from the bullet graze, taking some of his strength. Zeus's incessant barking wouldn't let up. He was running out of time.

Granger threw everything he had into the next strike.

The glass gave up the ghost.

He reached inside for the latch. Then dived in.

Dragging Charlie's unconscious body to him, he hauled her over his shoulder and ran for the incline. The fire was spreading along the SUV's frame. He had to move.

A hiss reached his ears.

A split second before the vehicle exploded.

Glass, metal and fire split in a thousand different directions from behind. He and Charlie had only made it halfway. Right in the explosion's path...

K-9 CONFIDENTIAL

NICHOLE SEVERN

Harlequin
INTRIGUE

To the men and women who've committed their lives
to fighting the drug crisis taking over our country.

ISBN-13: 978-1-335-45734-9

K-9 Confidential

Copyright © 2025 by Natascha Jaffa

Recycling programs
for this product may
not exist in your area.

Harlequin Enterprises ULC
22 Adelaide St. West, 41st Floor
Toronto, Ontario M5H 4E3, Canada
www.Harlequin.com

Printed in Lithuania

MIX
Paper | Supporting
responsible forestry
FSC® C021394

Nichole Severn writes explosive romantic suspense with strong heroines, heroes who dare challenge them and a hell of a lot of guns. She resides with her very supportive and patient husband, as well as her demon spawn, in Utah. When she's not writing, she's constantly injuring herself running, rock climbing, practicing yoga and snowboarding. She loves hearing from readers through her website, www.nicholesevern.com, and on Facebook at nicholesevern.

Books by Nichole Severn

Harlequin Intrigue

New Mexico Guard Dogs

K-9 Security
K-9 Detection
K-9 Shield
K-9 Guardians
K-9 Confidential

Defenders of Battle Mountain

Grave Danger
Dead Giveaway
Dead on Arrival
Presumed Dead
Over Her Dead Body
Dead Again

Visit the Author Profile page at Harlequin.com.

CAST OF CHARACTERS

Granger Morais—The former counterterrorism agent is haunted by everything Charlie and her family did to this country, and he's not up in arms to help her now. Only, the more he learns about her, the more he has reason to believe she's telling the truth about her innocence. And the more he needs to protect her.

Charlie Acker—She left her extremist family behind after losing her oldest sister in an attack she masterminded. And now the *Sangre por Sangre* cartel is on her trail. Her experience is exactly what the cartel needs to bring the organization back to life. Whether she agrees or not. She has only one place to turn: the counterterrorism agent who's been hunting for her all this time.

Socorro Security—The Pentagon's war on drugs has pulled the private military contractors of Socorro Security into the fray to dismantle the *Sangre por Sangre* cartel...forcing its operatives to risk their lives and their hearts in the process.

Henry Acker—Charlie's father has turned an entire New Mexico town into his own personal doomsday army, but his daughter's betrayal against the family is about to cost him everything. And he's not going down without a fight.

Ivy Bardot—She founded Socorro Security to battle the cartels the government can't touch. She makes the hard calls, but there's one she still can't let go of.

Chapter One

There had to be something here.

Charlie Acker shoved a stack of folded clothes to the other side of the dresser. The flashlight shook with the tremors in her hand. Unstable. "Come on. Come on."

Her fingernails scraped against cheap wood. Nothing in this drawer. She moved on to the next and the one after that. Coming up empty. Facing the rest of the bedroom, she took in the four-poster bed neatly made up with handmade quilts and crocheted throws. The bed itself had been carved by hand when her sister was old enough to sleep on her own. Charlie's heart squeezed too tight in her chest at the thought of her father giving it away to someone else. But that was how it worked in Vaughn, New Mexico. Nothing really belonged to the individuals living in this town. Everything was done for the benefit of the family.

"Talk to me, Erin." Charlie lowered the flashlight to keep from attracting outside attention. No matter how much she wanted answers, she couldn't risk exposing herself to the people of this town. Bad blood tended to stain more than anything else.

Her little sister had been dead for two days. Already

buried in the family cemetery, but there were still pieces of her here. In the knickknacks Erin had collected as a kid sitting on the bookshelf, even that gross old snail shell she'd picked up while weeding rows of corn when she'd been around five years old.

Charlie closed the distance between her and the nearest nightstand. In truth, she and Erin hadn't talked in years, but she'd known her sister suffered as much as she had after what they'd done.

After what they'd helped their father do.

There was no reason for her sister to start talking now, but that didn't mean Erin hadn't left something behind for Charlie to find. Because no matter how many years they'd gone without staying in touch, Erin had never given up on her. And no matter what anyone said, Charlie knew the truth. Erin hadn't died in a hunting accident, as she'd read in the papers.

Her sister had been murdered.

And she was going to find out why.

She slid onto the edge of the bed, careful not to let the box spring protest from her added weight. The nightstand drawer stuck on one side as she tried to slide it free. Her heart rocketed into her throat as she stilled. Listening. She wasn't supposed to be here. If the family—if her father—caught her within town limits, he'd make sure she never walked out again. Though her final resting place wouldn't be in the family cemetery. Not unless he'd reconsidered labeling her a traitor. Henry Acker: judge, jury and executioner. Had he been the last person Erin had seen before she died?

She couldn't think about that right now. Charlie pulled

a handmade bound journal from the depths of the nightstand. Loved, worn, soft with oils from her sister's hands. A ribbon marked her sister's last entry, and she set the flashlight on the nightstand at the perfect angle to wash across the pages. Thick, uneven pages pried away from each other as Charlie opened the journal and read the perfect cursive inside. It was all too easy to imagine Erin sitting right here, penning her final entry. Her sister would've taken her time. She would've made sure to document everything about her day to give an accurate picture of life in Vaughn at this very moment. Acting as historian had been Erin's job. Just as stocking and inventorying food and supplies and taking care of the house had been Charlie's growing up. And their eldest sister... She didn't want to think about that right now.

Tears burned in Charlie's eyes as a lavender flower—compressed between the pages—slipped free. Erin's favorite. There had to be a dozen in this journal alone.

She swiped a hand down her face. She was wasting time. Her father could realize she'd broken in any second. Shoving off the bed, Charlie knocked into the nightstand.

The flashlight hit the hardwood floor with a heavy thud.

A creak registered from somewhere else in the house. "Who's there? You're trespassing."

Heavy footsteps charged down the hallway. Growing louder with every step. Erin's bedroom door rattled. At least she'd thought enough ahead to lock it, just in case. But now she was out of time.

"Damn it." Charlie backed toward the window she'd

come through. She'd broken her only rule for coming back into this house. She'd let emotion distract her.

"You have three seconds to identify yourself." Her father's voice drove through her in a mixed battle of love and fear. "One. Two."

She clutched Erin's journal as she threaded a leg through the window. The flashlight rolled out of reach. She'd have to leave it.

The door crashed open.

It slammed against the wall.

A massive outline filled the doorframe, rifle aimed at her. "You've got a lot of nerve breaking into my house—" His booming voice caught. The gun wavered for just a moment as cold gray eyes narrowed on her through the darkness. "Charlie?"

Her fight-or-flight response pulled her through the frame in a panic. Gravity dragged her down, and Charlie hit the ground. Hard. Air knocked from her chest as she lost her hold on Erin's journal.

Those same heavy footsteps echoed from inside the house.

She had to get up. She had to run. Oxygen suctioned down into her lungs as she heard the front screen door scream on its old hinges. She clawed into the frozen ground to get her bearings and pushed to her feet. Stumbling forward, she scooped up the journal and pumped her legs as fast as she could.

A gunshot exploded overhead.

A warning shot.

It singed her nerves to the point her skin felt as though it were on fire. Spotlights flared to life as she ran down the dirt driveway. Wire fencing corralled her on either side to the end, and she cut to her left at the end. Her feet failed to absorb the impact of her boots against asphalt as she raced toward the neighboring farm where she'd left her car.

Another shot filled the night. Closer than before.

"Charlie! Stop where you are!" Henry Acker's voice cut through the night as clearly as one of the air raid sirens he'd had installed throughout town.

She wouldn't. She couldn't. Because no matter how much her body wanted to, the moment she surrendered, she'd lose any chance of proving her father and this town had a hand in the terrorist attack that'd left four people dead. *Ten years.* She'd been an outcast for every single one, had left her sister to die here alone. No. She wasn't going to stop. She was the only one who could fix this. Who could prove Erin had been murdered.

Charlie dared a glance over her shoulder to gauge the distance between them. Too close. Even in his late fifties, her father had kept himself ready for a war he'd prepared them to fight. The road inclined up, and the toe of her boot caught. She fell forward, hands out to catch herself.

Gravel cut into her palms and knees. The journal protected most of one hand, but the pain was still a shock to her system. She ordered her legs to take her weight.

A strong grip fisted the collar of her jacket and spun her around. She slipped the journal into her waistband a split second before she slammed into a wall of muscle. Forced to look up at the man she'd always feared. Feared to disrespect. To oppose. To disobey. Henry Acker had always been bigger than her. Harder. With no patience for the three girls he'd had to raise on his own. He pulled at her collar with one hand, leveling the rifle in the other straight toward the sky. "I told you what would happen if you came back here."

"I was never good at following orders, was I, Dad?" She tried to wrench out of his hold. Only she wasn't strong enough. She never had been. Not against him. "Never a good enough soldier for you."

The dark brown hair that'd once matched hers had whitened to the point he could've subbed for Santa at the mall. Heavy bags took up position under his eyes, as though he hadn't slept—not just in days, but weeks, months. Years. And she hoped like hell he'd suffered from whatever kept him up at night. "Hand it over. Whatever you took. I want it back."

"I don't know what you're talking about." Charlie rocketed her arm into his and thrust out of his hold. And he let her. She added a few feet of distance between them, but it wouldn't do a damn bit of good. Vaughn, New Mexico, wasn't some small town dying off from lack of tourism. It was a safehold. The birthplace of Acker's Army, where outsiders weren't allowed. This place? This was Henry Acker's kingdom, and she was nothing compared to the resources he held.

"You didn't break into your sister's room for nothing." Movement registered from her right as her father leveled the gun back on her. A shadow broke away from the tree line protecting her father's property. Then another from the left. He was having her surrounded. Cutting off her escape. "The journal. Hand it over or these two will take it from you by force."

Charlie took another step back. She could run, but there was no place in this world she could hide. Not anymore. "Why? Is it because you're afraid of what Erin wrote about you? About this place? Are you afraid she might expose you for what you really are?"

"And what is that, Charlie?" He countered her pitiful attempt to add distance between them.

She couldn't say the words. Couldn't accuse him, no matter how many times she'd thought of his dark deeds. Of what he'd made her and her sisters do. Her voice shook. "I know Erin didn't die in a hunting accident."

"Enough! I've given you a chance to cooperate, but as always, I'm going to have to force my hand with you." Her father's jaw flexed under the pressure of his back teeth, a habit he'd always had when she'd dared to defy his command. "Get the journal and bring her to my house. We have a lot to talk about."

The men waiting for her father's orders, like the good soldiers they were, moved in. She was out of time, out of patience waiting for Henry Acker to do the right thing. To prove he cared about her.

"I'm not going anywhere with you." Unholstering the small pistol stuffed on the front of her right hip, she took aim. At her father. Both men pulled their own weapons. "And I'm going to prove you had something to do with Erin's death. No matter how long it takes, Dad. Because she deserved better than you. Better than this place."

"You're making a mistake, Charlie." Seconds ticked by, each one longer than the last, as he leveled that bright blue gaze on her. "As always, you're only thinking of yourself instead of your family."

She took a step back, closer to the vehicle she'd stashed off the side of the road. Far enough away not to garner attention. One wrong move. That was all it would take, and she'd lose this game they'd been playing for so long. "Someone has to."

Charlie moved slower than she wanted to go, prying the driver's side door open. She lowered her weapon and collapsed into the seat as both gunmen ran to catch up. She started the engine as the first bullet punctured through the windshield. Low in her seat, she shoved the vehicle into Reverse and hit the accelerator, heart in her throat.

And knew Henry Acker was going to tear this world apart to find her.

"You've got to be kidding me." Former counterterrorism agent, Granger Morais, memorized the surveillance photos sprawled in a haphazard pile on the desk. It didn't take long. He'd been studying this subject for nearly a decade. The chestnut bangs that framed an oval face, dark eyes the color of coal, a sharp jawline that always seemed to be set in defiance. Granger checked the date on the surveillance. Yesterday. He rifled through the rest of the stack. "Where did you get these?"

Ivy Bardot—Socorro Security's founder and CEO herself—refused to give any hint as to how they were going to proceed with this new intel. This wasn't Socorro's case. His former life was coming back to haunt him, and she knew it. "Our source inside *Sangre por Sangre* sent them over an hour ago."

Sangre por Sangre. A bloodthirsty cartel hobbling on its last legs thanks to the men and women of Socorro who'd put their lives at risk to stop the infection spreading through New Mexico. Bombings, executions, drug smuggling, human trafficking, abductions, torture— there were no limits to the kind of pain the cartel could inflict, and they'd done so freely up until a year ago. Before the Pentagon had realized the threat and sent Socorro in to neutralize it. Now the cartel lieutenants were running with their tails between their legs. Hiding.

Granger reached out to test the glossy surface of the photos—to make sure this wasn't some kind of nightmare he'd gotten caught in for the thousandth time. Hesitation kept him from making contact. Ivy wasn't FBI anymore, but there was a reason she'd risen to the top of the Bureau's investigators in under a decade. She saw everything. He tensed the muscles in his right shoulder. "She wasn't at her sister's funeral three days ago. These were taken somewhere else. Who else knows?"

"You, me, our source." The weight of Ivy's gaze refused to let up. She was studying him, trying to break through his armor and get something that would tell her he was too invested in this, and hell, she was right. But he wasn't going to give her anything to use against him. "And we picked up radio chatter from Henry Acker."

The name sucker punched him harder than he expected. Henry Acker had a tendency to do that in the counterterrorism world. The unspoken decision-maker of a small angry militant group out of Vaughn, New

Mexico was a man with his fingers in a lot of pies, but not a whole lot of evidence to prove it. Someone who prided himself on getting away with murder by having others do his dirty work. Including his three daughters, two of whom had paid for his sins with their lives. And now Charlie was back. After ten years of hiding. Why? "You said these came from inside *Sangre por Sangre*. What would they want with a woman who blew up a pipeline ten years ago?"

"I don't know, but they're not wasting time trying to find her." Ivy shifted in her seat, the first real sign of life from Socorro's founder. "I've got a report that says they want to use her for something big. Something that may tip power back into *Sangre por Sangre*'s hands. Though my source couldn't tell me what, exactly."

"You want me to find her." It made sense. Granger was the only one on this team who had experience with homegrown terrorism and the painful aftermath people like Charlie Acker inflicted on bystanders who got in the way.

"There's a reason Charlie has chosen to show her face after all this time. If she's working for Daddy again, I want to know what Henry Acker is up to. Before we have another national incident on our hands," she said. "You've studied her behavior. You know what kind of resources she has at her disposal. Where would she go?"

Charlie Acker had managed to stay off his radar for a decade. There was no telling how many skills she'd picked up in that time or how many favors she'd called in, knowing she had to come back here. "Back in the day, I learned Charlie had a safe house outside of Vaughn.

From what I could tell, nobody in Acker's army knew about it. There was a code members had to stick to, especially the general's daughters. Loyalty is prized above all else. You stick with your kind, stay in the confines of town, but she managed to slide one by them. Bought it under an alias. She was careful whenever she went out there. Only reason I discovered the place was by accident. It's been abandoned since the bombing."

"You think she'd chance going back there?" Ivy asked.

"If she was desperate." He collected the photo from the top of the pile. A side-angle shot of Charlie Acker. "And something tells me if she's back, she's desperate."

"Take Zeus. Check it out." Ivy Bardot rose to her feet with a grace that shouldn't have been possible for a woman of her skill set and gathered the surveillance photos. "If Charlie's there, bring her in for questioning. I want to know what the hell *Sangre por Sangre* is up to before it's too late."

"You got it." Granger tossed the photo back on the top of the pile and headed for the door.

"And, Granger," Ivy said from behind. "Be careful."

He didn't have a response for that. The work he and his team did didn't come with kid gloves. More like as many blades as they could carry. They wedged themselves into unwanted dark places and pried secrets from shadows that never wanted to be exposed. They took down cartel lieutenants, demolished hideouts and drove evil back to where it came from—all to protect the innocent lives caught up in the violence.

He let the office door swing closed behind him and carved a path through the building's rebuilt maze of hall-

ways and corridors. White cracks still stretched down
black-painted walls as contractors worked to systematically patch the damage done by *Sangre por Sangre*'s
attack three weeks ago. Though Granger suspected it
would take more than drywall and mud to erase the past.

He rolled his aching shoulder back as he shoved
into his private room. Dr. Piel—Socorro's resident
physician—had gotten most of the bullet he'd taken during the attack, but not even she'd been able to get the last
piece of shrapnel out without disabling his arm for good.
He made his way to his private quarters and kicked the
door with the toe of his boot. Quiet. Too quiet.

Scanning his room, he stilled. Waiting. "I know
you're in here, and the fact you're being quiet makes
me think you got into something you shouldn't have."

A low groan registered from the other side of the bed.

Granger took his time as he rounded the built-in desk
and cabinets and the end of the messy bed he never bothered making anymore. He sat, noting a single camel-
colored leg sticking out from beneath the bed frame.
"Zeus."

The four-year-old bull terrier pulled his leg out of sight.

"I can see you." Keeping his weight off his right
shoulder, Granger slid to the floor to get an idea of what
his K9 had gotten into. "You ate the entire pack of beef
jerky, didn't you?"

Another moan and the scent of teriyaki confirmed his
suspicions.

Of all the K9 companions, he'd been the one to end
up with a bull terrier suffering from a binge eating disorder. Granger dragged a handful of wrappers from under

the bed. Bitten through. Not a single piece of meat left. "The only way you could've gotten to these is if you somehow learned how to fly, man. I'm going to have to install a camera in here."

He grabbed onto Zeus's back legs and pulled all eighty pounds of dog from underneath the bed. Granger scrubbed a hand along the K9's side. Yep. Twelve full beef jerky sticks. "We had a deal. One a day if you follow your diet."

A bright pink tongue darted out as though to communicate the dog wasn't the least bit sorry about anything other than the upset stomach that was coming his way.

"Come on. We've got an assignment." Granger shoved to stand and collected his gear. Within minutes, he and Zeus were descending to the garage. The K9 sniffed at the duffel bag with oversized black eyes. "No. These are my snacks. You already ate yours for the entire week."

The elevator pinged, and the shiny silver doors deposited them into Socorro's underground garage. Pain flared in Granger's shoulder as he left the confines of the elevator car. The bloodstains had been scrubbed out of the cement, but his memories of facing off against a dozen cartel soldiers alone would stay with him forever.

Zeus hopped into the rear of the SUV as Granger tossed his gear into the back. In seconds, noonday sun cut across the hood of the vehicle, and he directed them northeast. Toward Moriarty, a town with at least fifty miles distance between it and Vaughn. Granger had driven this route four times since the Alamo pipeline bombing, each time knowing he wasn't going to find what he was looking for. Each time not wanting to believe Charlie Acker had died along with her oldest sister in the terrorist attack that'd killed four others.

Except now they had proof she was still alive. That she was here in New Mexico. Granger's hands seemed to flex around the steering wheel of their own accord as the miles passed, Zeus's stomach growling the entire trip.

Breaking the borders of a town no one but two thousand people knew existed, he followed Route 66 to the opposite edge. Just far enough out of reach of nosy neighbors or unwanted guests. Scrub brush, cacti and dried grass swayed with the breeze, cutting across twenty-two acres purchased under a dead-end alias. In cash. Property taxes had been paid up front with a ten-year old money order sent directly to the city from a bank that no longer existed.

No way to trace it.

The house itself wasn't much. A single-level rambler that looked more like a double-wide trailer than a home. Bright teal wooden handrails stood out against the white siding and led up to a too-small covered porch. Bars on the windows. Oversized boulders funneling visitors in front of the largest window out front. Charlie Acker might've bought this place to escape Vaughn and her father's prepper army, but old habits died hard.

Granger threw the SUV into Park and loaded a bullet into the barrel of his sidearm before pushing out of the vehicle. Zeus huffed in annoyance as he hit the gravel driveway. Nothing but the sound of the wind reached his ears, but he was experienced enough to know silence hid all kinds of things from human perception. He took his time, moving slow to the north side of the house. The breaker box opened easily. All switches were active. The place had power.

No point in going for the front door. That was where she would've put most of her security measures. Granger and Zeus rounded to the back. He tested the laundry room door and twisted the knob. The door fell inward. No explosives. Nothing poised to spring out of the dark.

A low growl rumbled in Zeus's chest.

Granger ventured a single step inside, weapon raised.

The barrel of a gun pressed against his temple from the left. "Toss your weapons. Now."

Chapter Two

Her hand shook as she tried to keep the gun pressed against his head.

Charlie's nerves hiked into overdrive as the intruder's gun hit the dingy carpet with a hard thud. Seconds ticked off in her head. A minute. She wasn't sure how long she stood there or what she was going to do next. This wasn't part of the plan.

"I knew you were still alive. Even after all this time." His voice worked to counter the uneasiness clawing through her, but she wouldn't let it. Not this time. "This is usually the point where you close the door so no one sees you're holding a gun to my head and order me into the other room."

"This house is in the middle of twenty-two acres of land." She kicked the door closed, because that seemed to be the logical thing to do, all the while trying to keep both hands tight around the gun. The dog at his feet stared up at her as though expecting some kind of treat for parking his butt in her laundry room. "No one is going to see you coming and going."

"Does that mean I'm walking out of here alive?" he asked.

How could he ask that? After everything that'd happened, how could he still believe she'd been responsible for the deaths of those four people, of her *sister*, in that bombing? That she was a terrorist? Charlie forced herself to take a deep breath as next steps formed in her mind. "Into the living room. Straight ahead. You and your little dog, too."

"Might be hard to believe, but I'm familiar with the layout of this place." He followed her orders, moving forward through the tight hallway leading back into the laundry room from the main part of the house. "I've been here a few times."

She knew that. Security cameras had picked up his incessant search for clues each time he'd visited and relayed the live video to her phone. Despite her being thousands of miles away. After a few months, she'd come to crave that notification. To know that he was still thinking about her, that she hadn't been forgotten by the man tasked with bringing her in. Which didn't make a lick of sense.

She hadn't gotten those notifications in a long time.

Charlie maneuvered behind him, the gun now aimed at his spine. A thousand fantasies of this moment had kept her from going insane all these years. How she would approach him, what she would say. None of them seemed to fit the moment though. "What are you doing here, Agent Morais?"

"It's just Granger now." He pulled up short in the middle of the living room, turning as though to study his surroundings, but she was familiar with his way of working. How he liked to keep the threat in view. His

sidekick didn't seem to care she was holding a gun to
its owner though. Some guard dog. Afternoon sunlight
highlighted all the little details of his face. The shaggy
hair that always seemed to stay in place without effort,
the divots between his brows that'd creviced deeper over
the years, that long perfectly straight nose she'd come to
love. His eyes though. They'd somehow gotten darker.
Heavier. As though he'd lived two lifetimes in the span
of ten years. "Dropped the agent part soon after you
went off the radar."

He'd quit Homeland Security? It didn't matter. Charlie kept herself from shifting her weight, from giving
him any idea that her nerves were getting the best of her.
"That doesn't answer my question."

"I came here because I got a stack of surveillance
photos this morning. Of you." He said it so matter-of-
factly, without emotion, that the lack of inflection threatened to carve through her. "I don't know why you came
back. Frankly, I couldn't care less about what you're
doing here. I imagine the only reason your father hasn't
killed you is because he doesn't know about this place.
But considering how we got our intel, my boss seems to
think you might be a target of the local drug cartel, and
she wants to know why before a bunch of people die."

Her brain struggled to keep up with all the bits and
pieces of that statement. Charlie gave in to the need to
shift her weight onto her other leg. "Your boss? You said
you quit Homeland."

"I'm with Socorro Security," he said.

"Socorro." The word took some of the strength she'd
managed to summon over the past few seconds. Her arm

ached with the weight of the pistol in her hand. People like him trained for things like this, and while she'd been raised around guns and how to use them to defend what was hers, she wasn't like him. "You work for the private military contractor that declared war against the *Sangre por Sangre* cartel. You're one of their operatives."

"Despite what you might've thought when you disappeared, Charlie, the world moved on without you. *I* moved on. Only now, here you are, dragging me back into a life I fought to give up." Granger took his time facing her. Stepped into her, pressing his chest against the gun. "So we can do this one of two ways. You can come back to Socorro with me willingly to answer a few questions about your connection to *Sangre por Sangre* and what they want from you, or I can drag you out of here kicking and screaming. Either way, you're coming with me and Zeus."

The dog cocked his head to one side at the sound of his name.

"I didn't kill those people." Did he even care? Her mouth dried as memories she'd forced herself to relive every single day played at the back of her mind. "We were told there wouldn't be any civilians around. Sage set the explosives on the lower section of pipe while Erin worked ahead, but then we heard a vehicle approaching. It was dark. We couldn't see who it was, but it didn't matter. I told her to stop the countdown. She wouldn't listen. We argued. I had to knock her out, but when I ran to stop the explosives from going off, it was too late."

She could still feel the blistering fire and searing heat flash across her skin, driving beneath her clothing and burning her from the outside in. His gaze lowered to the lines of scarred, folded skin wrapping both forearms from beneath her jacket cuffs. "I tried to stop it."

"And yet you're the only one alive who can corroborate your version of events, Charlie." The hardness in his voice severed the final string of hope in her chest. This Granger Morais wasn't the man she'd studied—who she'd gotten to know, who she'd trusted—before the bombing.

He was right. Her oldest sister's body had been recovered at the scene, along with four other sets of remains. Erin had managed to escape, but she'd ended up six feet under back in Vaughn all these years later. Charlie had no proof of her story. Her father certainly wasn't going to step forward and incriminate himself. She had no home. She had no family. She had…nothing. Nothing except this moment with a man she never thought she'd see again. "It's the truth. I need you to believe that."

"The truth?" The deadpan tone in his voice suffocated the last of her optimism that they could work this out. "You're holding a gun to my chest, Charlie. You lied to everyone in your life, trying to convince them you were dead, including me. You had the chance to make this right since the moment that bomb went off, but you chose to run. You made the choice every single day to hide. What part of that is the truth?"

The survivor in her, the one who'd managed to keep herself off the radar, kicked her back into the present. She wasn't going anywhere with him. Not until she kept her promise to her sisters. "That was always your problem, Granger. Everything is so black-and-white for you, but that's not how the world works. You've been trained to think your assignments are the right thing to do, the right choice. But you don't know me anymore. And you have no idea what I'm willing to do to survive."

"Don't run, Charlie. You're only going to make matters worse," he said.

"I don't have a choice." She slammed her heel into the floor. The board she'd pried loose to once hide cash, a new identity and anything else she'd had to keep from her family collapsed under the weight. The other end shot up behind Granger. Charlie twisted away from him at the sound of impact and lunged for the front door. This wasn't a safe house anymore. She had to go.

Her hand met the doorknob. She wrenched the reinforced steel open and dashed into the New Mexico desert. Despite clear skies and a blazing sun, cold flooded through her from the change in temperature.

Heavy footsteps pounded through the house. Closer than she expected. But Charlie only had attention for the rental car stashed in the garage at the back of the house. The keys were already in the ignition in case she had to run. She could make it. She *had* to make it.

She pumped her legs harder, out of breath, as she turned the last corner. She didn't dare glance back to gauge the distance between her and Granger. It didn't matter. Exposing Henry Acker for the monster he was? That was all that mattered.

A low huff reached her ears.

Just before an impossible weight landed on her back.

The world tipped off balance as she collapsed forward. Her palms took most of the impact with bits of dirt embedded in the skin. Air exploded from her chest. Ten more feet. That was all that was left between her and the car. Charlie threw her elbow back to dislodge the weight on her back but met nothing but rolls of fat and fur. She tried to roll free. Only the mass of bull terrier refused to budge. She dug her toes into the ground and got a mouthful of dirt for her effort. It was no use. "For crying out loud, what does Granger feed you? I can't breathe."

"I warned you not to run. Zeus's favorite game is jump-on-the-bad-guy."

Is that what he really thought of her? That she was a bad guy?

"Get this thing off of me." Her ribs protested every inhale. This wasn't how she was supposed to die. She'd always imagined her final moments entailed facing off with her father and his army for not only ruining her life but her sisters'. Not suffocating beneath an overweight K9.

"Off." There was a bit of life in that single word, a kind of affection he'd once used when talking to her. "Now, are you coming back with me to Socorro willingly, or will Zeus have to sit on you again?"

She gasped for breath, rolling onto her back. "Please. I can't take anymore dog butt."

Granger centered in her vision. Nothing like the man she remembered all those years ago, and yet at the same time, everything she'd missed about this place.

Zeus penetrated her vision with a near smile as his tongue lolled to one side. And drooled down the side of her face.

A WAR HAD started behind his sternum. One between his personal life and the job he was supposed to do as a counterterrorism operative. Charlie Acker hadn't just betrayed her family when she'd dropped off the grid. She'd betrayed him and everything they'd done together.

Their secret plan to erode Henry Acker's immunity, to get her sisters as far from their father as possible, to free the people of Vaughn—it'd all gone up in flames with the pipeline she'd destroyed. He'd put his entire career on the line for her. And she'd merely used him to fake her death. All these years, the evidence hadn't lined up, but there was nowhere else for her to run now. If Charlie wanted to keep the new life she'd built, she'd have to rely on him.

"You found her." Ivy Bardot folded her arms over her chest, emerald green eyes dead set on the woman pacing the interrogation room.

It was an observational tactic. Leave a suspect or witness alone and study their behavior. Right now, the amount of tension in Charlie's shoulders told him she didn't like being kept in one place. Which meant she most likely hadn't let herself settle down in one location for long. Maybe a few weeks at a time. Never more than a couple months. Even after convincing everyone she'd died in that pipeline explosion, there was still a part of her that believed she could be found at any moment. And with good reason.

"Scarlett and Jones are searching the safe house as we speak." Socorro's security and combat experts wouldn't let anything slide by them. If Charlie was hiding something in that place, they were going to find it.

"She would've had to go by an alias all this time. I instructed them to start there. Give us a chance to see what she's been up to the past ten years. Maybe build a map of her activities."

"Why do I get the feeling you don't believe they're going to find anything?" Ivy's insight almost seemed supernatural, as though Socorro's founder could read the minds of her team. No matter what each of them were feeling or denying, Ivy saw right through every single one of them. She was a force to be reckoned with against congress, in the boardroom and her personal life. If that last one even existed.

"Henry Acker raised Charlie and her sisters to clean up after themselves. It's one of the reasons it's been impossible for us to pin any of these attacks on him or his army." Granger took in every movement, every shift from the interrogation room. The longer they left her inside, the higher chance she'd shut down. He had to time this right. Like a countdown on one of the bombs she used to handle, there was always a point of no return. "Based on what I saw of the safe house, she wasn't planning on staying there for long. No supplies, no more than a couple days of food. I've searched that property a dozen times. She wouldn't have left anything behind that could expose her. Like father, like daughter. She tried to wash it off, but there was dirt under her fingernails and smeared on her face."

"She dug something up. A new alias? Cash?" Ivy unwound her arms, turning toward him. "You're thinking she might still be in contact with Acker and his army?"

"I'm not sure." It would be easy to assume the connection, but he didn't have any proof. "Charlie has always resented her father's political leanings. Called him the homegrown terrorist nobody suspected. She faked her death after the pipeline explosion to get away from him. I can't imagine her willingly participating in his organization again."

"And how would you know that?" Ivy's attention attempted to dig deep past his armor. "From what I understood of your time with Homeland Security, you and Charlie Acker were never in contact. You were investigating Acker's Army from the outside. Or was there something missing from the reports you submitted?"

"No. Just a hunch." As Socorro's counterterrorism operative, Granger had spent the past four years helping Ivy build her own personal army to counter *Sangre por Sangre*. He'd risked his life, his morals and his trust in the people he served with, and he didn't owe her a damn thing. Certainly not an explanation into how little he'd included in his final report concerning the investigation into Charlie and her family.

He shoved through the interrogation room door with Ivy on his heels.

Charlie turned in expectation, instantly neutralizing any hint of the tension she'd let build over the past thirty minutes of isolation at the sight of Ivy at his back. Like the good terrorist she was supposed to be. "Who's this?"

"Ivy Bardot, Charlie Acker." He motioned between both women. One a monument of his past, the other his future. Granger slapped a file folder onto the table, and the surveillance photos Ivy had shown him this morning spilled out. "Ivy is the founder and CEO of Socorro.

You're here because we got these from an inside source of the *Sangre por Sangre* cartel."

Charlie moved—far too gracefully—to pick up the top photo of the file. No sign of distress. Nothing to suggest she was taking this as seriously as they were, apart from the loss of color in her cheeks. Good. She needed to know what kind of mess she'd left behind and just how far the cartel would go to survive. "Who's your source?"

"That's none of your concern, Ms. Acker," Ivy said. "Now I've been patient, but I'm afraid we don't have much time before *Sangre por Sangre* traces you back to Socorro, and I can't risk a head-on attack at the moment. So let's just get everything out in the open, shall we? You were responsible for the destruction of the Alamo pipeline ten years ago."

Charlie's gaze cut to Granger, but he wasn't going to help her out of this one. Despite her claims of innocence, of arguing with her sister and trying to stop those explosives from going off, evidence never lied. It'd been her blood investigators had collected from the scene. Preserved with that of five others. She refocused on Ivy, pulling her shoulders back. "Yes."

Surprise pricked at the back of Granger's neck. Then turned ice-cold in his veins. No matter what the evidence said, he'd wanted to believe her. To believe that she wouldn't have gone along with Henry Acker's plan to sabotage the government and everyone he considered a threat. Then again, he hadn't really known her, had he? She'd been a suspect, then a source. Then something far more. All in the span of weeks.

"I designed the mission. My sisters and I were instructed to set charges at two intervals along the south-west curve of the pipeline outside the town of Bennett." Slow breathing exaggerated the rise and fall of Charlie's shoulders, to the point Granger was convinced she was forcing herself to keep her inhales and exhales at an even pace. To prove she was in control. "My younger sister, Erin, took care of the first one. Sage was in charge of setting the second. I was assigned to be the lookout."

"At Henry Acker's instruction," Ivy said.

Charlie notched her chin higher. A visible struggle twitched the corner of one side of her mouth. A fight between defending herself or defending the man who raised her. Henry Acker was responsible for three separate attacks aimed at government property, like the one carried out at the Alamo pipeline. That they knew of. Dozens of innocent lives taken. Massive amounts of financial damage, not to mention the installation of fear across the state, but in the end, he would always be Charlie's father. She tented her fingers over the top surveillance photo. "That was a long time ago. What does any of this have to do with a drug cartel?"

"That's what we're trying to find out," Granger said. "*Sangre por Sangre* isn't in a position to waste resources at the moment. What's left of the cartel is scattered and in hiding after they attacked Socorro head on three weeks ago, but this surveillance tells us they've got their sights on you. Why?"

Charlie folded her arms across her chest. Not in defense. He knew as well as anyone the kind of rigorous combat training she'd been put through as a kid. No. She was hiding something. Trying to keep him at a distance. "How should I know?"

"Because you're the only Acker daughter still alive." Ivy leveled the statement almost like an accusation. The last connection to the inside of Acker's Army. "*Sangre por Sangre* might be on its last legs, but they still have resources we can't even begin to imagine. It's possible whoever is targeting you knows you and your sisters were involved in the Alamo pipeline attack and want something specific from you." Ivy slid her hands into her blazer pockets. "Or this could have nothing to do with you and everything to do with getting to your father. Through you."

"What do you mean?" Charlie asked.

"Henry Acker has continued his mission since you've been gone, including two other attacks in the state." Granger leveraged his weight against the oversized conference room table. "Both were aimed at undermining the government, and by doing so, Acker's Army has proven themselves a real threat. *Sangre por Sangre* may be taking notice. Might even use his daughters to get to manipulate or influence him."

"Wait." Charlie released her hold on herself. A physical calm washed over her features, a stillness that could only be achieved through years of training. "You think this cartel could be involved in my sister's murder?"

"Murder?" Granger stood a bit taller as he cut his attention to Ivy and back. "As far as Vaughn PD and the media are concerned, Erin died in a hunting accident."

Charlie's mouth parted on a shaky inhale. The first real sign that something was very wrong.

"That's why you came back." Granger should've seen it before now. There was no plausible situation he'd been able to think of that would explain her return to New Mexico, and yet here she was, after all this time. The muscles down his back pulled tight as a chain reaction of sympathy and anger and grief charged through him. Erin Acker didn't have the same views of her father and his anti-government protests as her sister, but Charlie had loved her sister all the same. Even tried to get her out of Acker's Army before the attack on the pipeline. Only she hadn't been fast enough. "You don't believe your sister's death was an accident."

"No. I don't." Charlie locked away the vulnerability that'd taken over for a brief moment. "And I'm not going anywhere until I find who killed her."

Chapter Three

This place was so cold.

Not in the sense she expected. Just...empty. Lonely. Though she should've been used to that by now. North Dakota, Montana, Utah, parts of Colorado. She hadn't let herself stay in any of them long or get to know anyone. She couldn't take the risk with her father and his army on the hunt, but Socorro's headquarters felt even more isolating. Like a prison.

Charlie lowered herself onto the edge of the mattress. The bedroom Ivy Bardot and Granger had stuck her in looked comfortable enough, but there was a reason she'd survived this long. She never took anything at face value. What was this place? A private military contractor and bed-and-breakfast? Her stomach growled at the thought. She hadn't stopped moving since she'd crossed state lines.

Pulling Erin's journal from the back of her waistband, she flipped to the first page. She could still recall the expression on her father's face as she'd sped away last night, but disappointment came with the job of being that man's daughter. And Henry Acker was the kind of person to never forget a grudge.

He would punish her if he got the chance. Just as he had when she'd been a kid. Whine about how much her body hurt after training all day? Run ten laps around the farm. Fail to clean her rifle that week? Stand outside in below freezing temperatures until her fingers no longer worked.

At the time, she hadn't considered how wrong those punishments had been. How...traumatic. She'd simply seen them as a way to become a better daughter, facing them head-on and believing her father was only doing it because he loved her. In reality, all he'd wanted was another soldier to add to his ranks.

Tears prickled at her eyes as she traced the well-loved leather of her sister's journal. Erin and she used to write notes to each other in a journal exactly like this. They'd designed a secret code only they knew. If their father ever found it, he wouldn't know what to make of it, because they'd been the only ones who'd had the key to decipher the message. She missed that. The cover wasn't new. It'd once belonged to their mother. Erin had reused it a hundred times as she recorded events throughout their childhood, a much-needed habit the Acker matriarch had instilled in only her youngest child. Charlie had always claimed to have better things to do. Learning the latest war-game strategy, checking the perimeter of the farm for the dozenth time, running inventory on emergency supplies. Though there were times she wished she'd journaled. For evidence. But maybe there was something in these pages that could help. Could point her in the right direction.

She flipped through the notebook. The contents were

routinely swapped out for new pages whenever Erin filled the latest journal up. This one was half-full of coded handwriting, with the final entry dated four days ago. The day of Erin's death. Only this code wasn't the one they'd created as kids. This was something more... complicated.

"Thought you could use something to eat," that deep voice said.

She hadn't heard him come in, too distracted by Erin's final words. Rookie mistake. If Henry Acker had witnessed her slip, she'd have to dig ditches until her hands bled. "How long have you been standing there?"

He moved slowly, as though approaching a wild animal, and, in a sense, that was exactly what she was. Feral, without a home, alone. Granger maneuvered to her side and set a tray of what looked like sweet-and-sour chicken and white rice on the bed. The scent alone was enough to remind her she hadn't been taking care of herself the past few days. Hell, he could probably smell the three days' worth of sweat and tears on her. "Not long."

She wouldn't get anything else out of him. Not unless it was on his terms. That was one of the things she'd liked about him the most when they first met, one thing that they'd had in common. It wasn't much, but it'd been more than she'd had with anyone else. "Thank you."

He added a good amount of distance between them. At least as much as the room would give him. "Is that Erin's?"

"I took it from her room last night." Her attention was split between her need for answers in the journal and her need for calories. Her father would be so disappointed to learn her stomach was winning the fight.

"You went back to Vaughn." A concern she recognized from the old days tinted his words and set her nerves on red alert. They weren't friends. They weren't even acquaintances at this point. "And you lived to tell the tale."

"I saw him. My father." Charlie held herself back from shoving in more food than her mouth could take, simply pulling the tray onto her lap. She stabbed at a hefty piece of chicken covered in sauce and sticky rice, and her mouth watered. Chinese food had always been her favorite. It'd been such a delicacy compared to the canned and dehydrated foods she'd grown up on. Had Granger remembered that? "He caught me, tried to drag me back. Even had a couple of his lieutenants try to bring me in."

"But you escaped." Was that a hint of respect she sensed in his tone?

"I didn't have a choice." The bite of sweet-and-sour chicken coated her tongue and sent the first real glimpse of relief through her. One bite. That was all it took to lose herself in the experience, to the point this place, the cartel, her father—none of it existed. All that was left was this sweet-and-sour chicken and Granger. A laugh rushed up her throat. "Thank you for this. I haven't had something this good in a long time. Not a whole lot of options while you're in hiding. Going to restaurants or anyplace with security cameras was too big a risk"

"And yet the cartel got you on surveillance," he said.

"I was careful." She was getting full, but she didn't

dare stop eating for fear she'd never have this small joy
again. "Those photos you have of me must be from street
cameras, because I sure as hell didn't put myself at risk.
Not after everything I worked to keep."

He didn't seem to have an answer for that. Or he'd decided she wasn't the person to trust with one, and that…
hurt.

Deep. Where she thought she'd buried everything
about the past and him. It hadn't been easy. Granger
Morais had been a big part of her life there for a while.
In more ways than one. But she couldn't think about
that right now. Erin was dead. She needed to know why.
Charlie stared down at the mix of vegetables, sauce and
chicken, no longer captive to her appetite. This thing
that'd brought them together was more important than
either of them. "My goals haven't changed, Granger. I
still believe my father and his army are a massive threat. I
want to tear them apart."

"Then why did you leave?" That last word seemed to
catch in his throat. "We had a plan. You signed an agreement with the US government, Charlie, and you backed
out by running. The feds have your name and picture at
the top of their terrorism list, and there isn't anything
I can do about that. If Homeland realizes you're alive,
they'll do whatever it takes to put you behind bars and
keep you there for a very long time."

"I know." She'd lived with the reality of what she'd
done every day since crawling away from that explosion. And not without scars. "You trusted me, and I…
I got scared."

"Scared." Granger turned away from her. "From what

I remember, there isn't a damn thing in this world that scares you, Charlie. You were willing to give us intel on your father and the people who raised you, knowing exactly what they would do to you if they found out. Hell, you weren't even supposed to be there the night of the attack."

"I thought…" An uncomfortable pit weighed heavy in her stomach, and suddenly Charlie wished she hadn't eaten before having this conversation. There were still pieces of the past that could get to her. No matter how far she tried to run. Tossing the meal he'd brought her back onto the tray, she slid her clammy palms down her jeans and shoved to stand. Her sister's journal bounced with the absence of her weight on the mattress. "You know what? It doesn't matter what I thought. The only reason I'm here is because Erin is dead, Granger. And you're right. We had a deal. I gave you everything you needed to take down my father a decade ago and get her away from him, but it seems you didn't hold up your end of the deal either. So here we are. You said this cartel you've been fighting might have something to do with her death, to get to my father, and now they're gunning for me. I want to know everything you know, and I want to know now. Who killed my sister?"

Mountainous shoulders pulled tight and accentuated his chest. Granger didn't look strong in the sense of the other male operatives she'd clocked in the building. He didn't need hours in the gym or gallons of protein powder to incapacitate a threat, though she knew he took care of himself. No. He had something far more dangerous packed into his lean six-foot-two frame. Something far more valuable: hard-to-come-by skills the US government wouldn't have wanted to lose. Strategy, foresight, high deductive reasoning. Not to mention extensive training in surveillance and combat. Everything a counterterrorism agent would need to save the world. In truth, he'd intimidated her the first time they'd met. Though she could argue they were evenly matched in many respects, Granger Morais always seemed to surprise her in the best of ways.

"What makes you think Erin didn't die in a hunting accident as the coroner reported?" His voice had slipped back into that near-whisper—too calm, too distant.

"Because Erin was the best damn hunter our father has ever trained. She knew her way around a rifle better than any of us. It was one of the reasons Sage and I always felt she was the favorite." Which left the question of whether her father had anything to do with his third daughter's death. Had he grown so callous, so vengeful, that he'd sacrifice one daughter to get to the other? Had he known Charlie had survived the explosion before she'd broken into the house last night? He'd seemed genuinely surprised to see her, but Henry Acker was a strategist. Never one to show his hand until the perfect moment. "Erin could hit a buck from five-hundred yards dead between the eyes. There's no way she made a mistake and got herself killed. Something else is going on here."

"Could someone have killed her to draw you out of hiding?" he said.

Charlie kept herself from folding her arms, from giving any kind of clue as to what was going on in her mind.

She'd already come to a conclusion. The answer to that could be all right there in Erin's journal. She just needed to decode Erin's final days. Find the decipher key that would unlock the whole entry. "It crossed my mind."

"All right." Granger crossed the room to the built-in bureau taking up one side of the room. He popped the cabinet open and hit a series of numbers on the gun safe inside. The door swung open, and he pulled a sidearm from inside. "Let's go test that theory."

THIS WAS THE stupidest idea he'd ever considered.

Setting foot in Vaughn, New Mexico, could only end in a death sentence now that he wasn't employed by the federal government. Henry Acker had all the rights and reasons to shoot him on sight. And all the answers as to why the *Sangre por Sangre* cartel had targeted Charlie.

She hadn't said a word from the passenger seat. Though Granger could argue she wasn't really taking in the sights out the window either. Her hands were too tense, fingernails digging into her knees with every mile gained on Vaughn.

He checked on Zeus through the rearview mirror. The overstuffed K9 was asleep across the back seat after having gorged himself on the leftovers of Granger's lunch.

"You don't have to go in with me." It wasn't the first time he'd made the offer. "I've done this a few times. I'm kind of good at gathering intel and working my way into places I'm not supposed to be."

"You think my father is going to just let you walk up to his front porch?" Charlie graced him with one of those rare smiles, as though the thought of him taking a bullet center mass entertained her, before she turned back to the window. "You'll be dead the second you cross the town border unless I'm with you."

"And if he's not in the welcoming mood?" Granger tried not to let his hands tighten around the steering wheel at the thought. Not of him being taken down in action. He'd signed on with Socorro knowing exactly what he was getting himself into and was carrying a piece of a bullet around to prove it. But Charlie was a civilian despite her militaristic upbringing, and there was a difference between thinking she'd been dead all this time and watching her take her last breath beside him.

"We always knew there was a chance he'd kill us for working against him." Her inhale shook more than he imagined she'd intended. Fear did that to a person. Took everything they believed in and turned it against them. Charlie might believe some part of her father still loved her enough not to shoot her on sight, but there was still a high chance neither of them would walk out of Vaughn alive. "I guess now we'll find out if that's true."

"He didn't shoot you when you broke into the house last night," he said. "I'd take that as a good sign."

"I didn't really give him the chance." She pressed her shoulders back into the seat, tense. "I might hate everything he stands for and the way he brainwashes people into following his beliefs, but the only reason I was able to disappear was because of the things he taught me. How to live off the grid, which high calorie foods would serve me better in the long run, how to recognize if I'm being followed. In some weird way, I owe my life to him."

Granger didn't know what to say to that, what to think. Trials had a way of preparing the sufferer. Some better than others. "Where have you been living?"

"Here and there. Nowhere longer than a couple weeks at a time. I took odd jobs for cash and stayed in hotels. I couldn't take the risk of...wanting more," she said. "North Dakota, Montana. Visited Washington state for a while. They were nothing like this place. Everything here is so...harsh. And up there, I felt like myself. Surrounded by trees and the smell of dampness from the rain. It was like I'd become someone else. Almost enough to convince me I could escape what I'd done."

"Yeah. I bet it was easy to pretend after convincing everyone who cared about you that you were dead." Granger regretted the words the moment they escaped his mouth. This wasn't about him. This wasn't about them and what they'd lost that night. The cartel had plans for Charlie, and it was his job to figure out what they were. Nothing else mattered. He was here to do a job. Nothing more.

Charlie swung her gaze toward him. "I'm sorry. For everything, Granger. If I'd stuck to the plan, maybe none of this would've happened. Maybe Sage and Erin would still be alive."

"So why didn't you?" Dirt kicked up alongside the SUV as he maneuvered onto a one-way unpaved road that would take them straight into the heart of Vaughn. He had to tell himself to press against the accelerator to keep himself from letting the vehicle roll to a stop. To give them more time. "Why didn't you stick to the plan?"

"Because I was afraid." She hadn't shied away from

him this time, the weight of her attention solid and vulnerable. "We started out needing something from each other. You needed me to help you take down my father, and I needed you to get me and my sisters out of Vaughn safely, but then it became something more than that. We became something more. I was in love with you, Granger."

That final statement gutted him more efficiently than a blade.

"I was willing to give up everything we were working for if you had just asked. To the point I actually hoped you would, but those words never came. You wanted me to go through with my end of the deal, and I needed you to hold up yours," she said. "The night of the pipeline attack, Sage confronted me. She knew about us. I don't know how, but she was ready to expose me to our father. Tell him everything I'd done. That was what we were arguing about before the charges went off. She accused me of destroying our family, when all I'd wanted to do was save it. And she told me you were just using me to get to Dad. That the moment I was done being useful, you would throw me behind bars with the rest of Acker's Army."

Hell. An ache swelled along his jaw from the pressure on his back teeth. Granger kept his attention forward, but his entire nervous system had honed on Charlie. On the pain in her voice, in her words. "You believed her."

"Yeah, Granger. I believed her." She settled back into staring out the passenger side window. "So I did what I thought I had to do to protect myself, and I never looked back."

Silence cut through the SUV, apart from the crunch of

dirt and rock beneath the vehicle's tires. A barbed wire fence came into view along the right side of the road, signaling Vaughn's western border. Granger took his foot off the accelerator, and the SUV slid to a stop mere feet from crossing that sacred, invisible line.

Charlie moved to get out of the vehicle.

"I was in love with you too." Granger needed to make that clear. That what'd happened between them hadn't been part of some grand scheme to get inside Acker's Army and her pants. There were rules against relationships between agents and their confidential informants, but he hadn't been able to keep himself in check. Not when it came to her. In a sense, the forbidden nature of their relationship had made it all the more exciting, but those initial feelings of lust had quickly dissolved and left something more real behind. "Your sister was wrong. Whatever she convinced you of was a lie, Charlie, and when I got word you were involved in the attack, I wasn't angry you hadn't held up your end of the deal. I was worried I'd lost you."

Zeus's stomach growled in the silence and seemed to knock Charlie back into the present.

Her attention cut out the windshield, and the tension she'd managed to lose over the past few minutes returned. "They're here."

Granger diverted his senses to the threat coming down the road. Dirt puffed around three trucks charging straight for them. For a militaristic operation, Henry Acker could use some new wheels. His training took over then, and Granger whistled low to wake Zeus. The bull terrier launched himself out of the vehicle and followed on Granger's heels.

He and Charlie moved as one toward the SUV's front bumper. Ready for anything. They met as a team for the first time in over a decade. "You armed?"

"Don't worry about me." Long brown hair blew back over her shoulders as she faced the oncoming storm. Just as he remembered. "My father isn't going to let anyone but himself kill me, if that's how he chooses to end this. He'd consider it the coward's way out, and Henry Acker is no coward."

Granger fought the urge to unholster his weapon. Acker owned the entire town, the land, the buildings, the people who resided here. This was all private property that'd been incorporated through political pressure and a whole lot of personal funds. One wrong move and he'd lose any chance of figuring out *Sangre por Sangre*'s intentions for Charlie.

Zeus's growl vibrated into Granger's leg.

"Steady. You won't be flattening anyone today, mutt," he said.

"You really need to put that dog on a diet." Charlie took a clear step forward, crossing the demarcation line, raising her hands in surrender as the lead truck skidded to a stop. The two vehicles behind it each veered off to both sides, one right, the other left. Driver's side doors fell open, and a handful of pretend soldiers splayed into formation, taking aim.

"Hold it right there! You're trespassing on private property."

"Get down on your knees and put your hands behind your heads."

Charlie cut her gaze back over her shoulder, locking Granger in her sights. A single nod preceded her agreement. She'd warned him of the ways in which Henry Acker would exert his dominance over them. This was just the beginning. She dropped onto one knee, then the other, and interlaced her hands behind her head.

One of the soldiers centered his weapon on Granger. "I said on your knees! Or can't you hear?"

Granger had faced all kinds of danger in his pursuit of terrorists like these men. The ones who followed orders blindly for a cause that had nothing to do with them. The masterminds who disregarded the lives devoted to them as nothing more than ants under their boots. Like the *Sangre por Sangre* lieutenants he and his team had taken on. These men weren't more than thirty, some even younger. They had their entire lives ahead of them, and yet Henry Acker had somehow convinced them to fight against the very country that'd been born into.

"Granger. It's the only way to get to my father." Charlie's voice carried to him. They had one shot at this. They had to play their cards right.

He lowered to his knees.

The soldier who'd ordered Granger down rushed forward.

Charlie reached for him with one hand. "No!"

The butt of the soldier's rifle connected with Granger's temple.

And the world went black.

Chapter Four

Pricks of sunlight pierced through the bag over her head, but not enough to gauge where they were taking her.

Charlie stumbled forward at a push from behind, only managing to catch herself by taking small steps. They'd secured her wrists behind her back with zip ties. Didn't they realize she'd been brought up just like them? It would take more than zip ties to hold her back. Small rocks worked into her boots as they walked. "You didn't have to knock him out."

"Mouth closed. Keep moving." It was the same soldier, the one who'd taken charge and clocked Granger with the butt of his rifle. The distinct sound of dragging punctured through the pound of her heart. They had to carry Granger now that he was unconscious. And where was Zeus?

A whine pierced her ears. The bull terrier was struggling without orders it seemed.

Charlie tried to distract herself from the sick feeling that'd taken hold as Granger had hit the ground. Her fists tugged against the zip ties, and she couldn't contain the laugh sticking in her chest. Men like this particular soldier didn't get to take charge. Not as long as her father was alive, and Daddy didn't like to share the glory. She turned her head where she thought the soldier might be standing. "I'm going to remember you long after Henry Acker uses you up and discards you like the ones who've come before you."

Pain speared across her back, and she launched forward. The ground rushed to meet her faster than she expected. Her shoulder caught the brunt. It was a miracle she managed not to hit her head. Something heavy lodged into her ribs and rolled her onto her back. A foot.

"I told you to keep your mouth shut." Rough hands wrenched her to her feet and guided her a few more steps.

They were coming up on her father's barn. Because it didn't matter that they'd put a bag over her head to keep whatever secrets they had safe. She'd been born here, learned to walk here, ran laps around this property a thousand times. Every inch of Vaughn had been carved into her brain a long time ago. She knew exactly where they were headed.

The crunch of gravel beneath boots slowed. A heavy thud registered from her left as the soldier at her back pulled her to a stop. Despite the full-blown sun overhead, a chill took hold along her spine. November in the desert had always been magical to her. When nature seemed to freeze for a time, when she got a break from working the land and the livestock didn't need her as much. It was a time of gratitude in her house. For what they'd accomplished and what they'd been blessed with throughout the season. When Henry Acker seemed more like the father she remembered than the hardened extremist he'd become after her mother's death.

"Looks like we got visitors." The gravelly voice accompanied a series of footsteps. Close but with enough distance to counter an attack. Just like he'd taught her.

"Trespassers, sir."

"Caught them at the edge of town, the end of Magnolia."

"Take the hoods off," her father said.

Stinging pain ripped across her skull as the soldier who'd shoved her fisted the bag over her head and pulled. She automatically winced against the onslaught of blinding sun and didn't see the next strike coming. The soldier launched his rifle into the back of her knee, and she collapsed.

"Don't touch her!" The words were more predatorial than human. Shuffling kicked up dirt onto her hands and forearms as she caught sight of Granger fighting for release between two other soldiers. A fist rocketed into his gut and took him down to his knees. "I'm going to make you pay for that, you son of a bitch."

Henry Acker didn't need to see her face to recognize her, but Charlie got to her feet to face him all the same. To prove she could. The soldier at her back moved to subdue her again. Her father raised a hand to warn him off.

She breathed in the scent of dried-out hay, the odor from the chickens and the cooling scent of dropping temperatures as the sun reached the second half of the sky. So many memories battled for dominance here. Some good, some bad. But all of them hers. All of them combining to make her into the woman she was today. "Hi, Daddy."

A wall of nervous energy hit her from behind. The

soldier who'd brought her in hadn't recognized her. She wasn't surprised, given the ten or more years between them.

"The prodigal daughter returns." Henry Acker let a half smile of amusement crease one side of his mouth as he wiped his hands clean with a work towel. Black smudges spread across the strong hands she'd once trusted to protect her. Never one to shy away from the work that needed to be done. One of the tractors must be out of commission. He motioned to Granger. "Who's your friend?"

"Nobody you need to concern yourself with." Charlie managed a glance at Granger. A dark bruise had already started forming alongside his face, but she couldn't see any swelling. A concussion? "But I'd watch out for the dog, if I were you. He likes to sit on people."

Zeus cocked his head to one side and parked his butt on the ground. Ever the loyal companion.

"Granger Morais." Her partner wrenched out of the hold of both soldiers working to contain him.

"Morais. I remember the name. Homeland Security, right? You investigated the death of my firstborn after that attack on the Alamo pipeline. Sage." Henry absently nodded. "You brought a federal agent into my town?"

Her father closed the distance between him and Charlie. He stuffed the rag in the back pocket of his worn jeans. That all-too-familiar shiver of his authority raced through her as he reached for her. Charlie tried to dodge his attempt at contact, but there was nowhere for her to run this time. He gripped her chin, giving her a full view of his aging face. "You're bleeding."

Acid charged into her throat at his touch.

"I fell." Half-truths. That was how she'd managed to survive in Vaughn for so long while she and Granger strategized on how to dismantle Acker's Army. The more honest she could be when talking to her father, the higher chance he'd continue to trust her. Charlie maneuvered out of his hold.

"I see." Her father unholstered the gun at his right side, letting it dangle in his hand for a moment. "Do I have you to thank for that, Johnny?"

"I asked her to keep her mouth shut, sir." Johnny. The soldier who'd bagged her and knocked Granger unconscious shifted his feet. He held onto the strap of his rifle as though to prove he belonged. "She refused."

A low laugh rumbled through Henry Acker as he circled behind her. Charlie knew what was coming next, and she didn't have the stomach to watch despite Johnny's treatment of her. "Nobody lays a hand on my daughter."

The first strike was the loudest, and a cringe cut through Charlie. Johnny's cry didn't come close to the sound of the butt of her father's weapon against his skull. She tried to focus on Granger, on the rise and fall of his chest, of the pattern of the bruise on his face, but it didn't help. The second strike accompanied a thud of the soldier's body hitting the ground. No cry this time. Granger turned away from the attack. The third strike to Johnny's head sounded more wet than any preceding it.

Zeus set his head against his master's leg.

Then silence.

Heavy breathing reached her ears as her father handed

off his weapon to one of the other men. He wiped his head and hands with the same work towel he'd used while fixing his tractor. As though it'd never happened.

"Was that really necessary?" Granger didn't understand the rules here, that he didn't have any authority or rights. Vaughn police were controlled by Henry Acker. The mayor was controlled by Henry Acker. Anything and everything that happened in this town went through him, and there was nothing anyone could say or do to change that.

"He's alive, which is more than he deserves." Henry motioned for two of the other soldiers to clean up the mess he'd made, and they collected Johnny's body and hauled him out of sight. "Now, Charlie, considering you brought Agent Morais onto my property, I'm starting to think you're not here to apologize for making me think I lost two daughters in that pipeline explosion. When you broke into my house last night, you accused me of having something to do with Erin's death. Is that what this is, Charlie Grace?" He motioned to Granger. "You here to have Agent Morais bring me in?"

First and middle-named. It'd always been a warning for when she'd crossed a line as a kid. Only now it seemed to have a much stronger effect, despite her years of emotional and physical distance. "Erin wanted out, Dad. She'd been trying to leave for years, but you just wouldn't let her. You wouldn't let any of us. Sage had to die to get away, I had to fake my death and run, and Erin—"

"Erin died in a hunting accident. Just like the coroner said." A slip of her father's eyes gave her the answer she craved, and her heart squeezed too tight in her chest. He scrubbed at the same spot on his hands, a little too hard.

"A coroner who would write whatever you told him to write in his report." The zip ties were cutting deeper due to the tension in her hands and arms. "Because that's how it works around here, doesn't it? Everyone here worships you. Every word out of your mouth is gospel. No matter how many lives have to be sacrificed, nobody is allowed to question you for the good of the cause."

"I keep them safe. They know that, and they reward me with their service." Her father shoved the towel back into his jeans and headed for the barn, leaving her and Granger zip-tied in the middle of the most dangerous place on earth. "Let them go. See if they can make it to the town border alive."

Bastard.

But she wasn't finished. After all these years, she finally had the courage to stand up for herself, for her sisters. "You brainwash them, just like you brainwashed your own daughters, and look what happened. Two of them are dead, and the other is the target of a drug cartel. Because of you and your extremist bullshit."

"Drug cartel?" Henry Acker turned to face her, years of age, any hint of grief he'd shown and some color melting away. In front of her was the man she'd wanted to love her more than anything—to choose her over his cause—who had come up short every chance he got. "Don't come back, Charlie. There's nothing left here for you."

"I'm not leaving until I find out what happened to my sister." She squared her shoulders, feeling stronger than ever. Maybe it had everything to do with Granger at her side or the fact she really had nothing left to lose, but she would take it. All of it. "You don't scare me anymore, Dad. I'm going to find out the truth. In the end, you're going to pay for everything you did to us."

"You've been warned, Charlie," Henry said. "Get them out of my town."

His HEAD POUNDED harder than it should.

Sundown was in less than twenty minutes.

Henry Acker walked into his barn without another glance in their direction. The Acker patriarch had set the rules. Breaking them would bring a rain of hell on earth. Granger had witnessed it firsthand. But he'd gotten what they'd come for. Confirmation. Henry Acker had paused at the mention of *Sangre por Sangre*. Might as well told them right then and there he knew exactly what the cartel wanted with Charlie.

"Let's go, princess." Another one of Acker's soldiers shoved Charlie forward, but she managed to stay on her own two feet.

"I told you. I'm not going anywhere." Charlie broke out of the zip ties as if the plastic was mere sewing thread. And hell if that wasn't one of the sexiest things he'd ever seen. She turned on the soldier at her back and rammed her fist into his face. No, wait. That was the sexiest thing he'd ever seen.

The man hit the ground. Out cold.

Granger wrenched his wrists down as hard as he could and snapped the zip ties loose. He turned on the escort behind him and knocked the soldier out cold. Rubbing at his wrists, he stared into the barn. Hell, they were in the middle of enemy territory. "An abduction, a beating and a death threat all in one day. You sure know how to show a fellow a good time. Hadn't expected to meet the parents so soon though."

"It could've been a lot worse." Johnny obviously hadn't known who he was dealing with when he'd dragged Charlie into town. She turned that dark gaze on him. "He could've strip-searched you like the first boy who dared ask me on a date. Get their feet."

They dragged each soldier away from the front of the barn and behind a wall of bailed hay. Not ideal but the best option they had.

"Guess I should be grateful." His laugh took him by surprise. "All right. So we're in the middle of a hostile town with twenty minutes until the sun goes down. What now?"

"We make those twenty minutes count." Charlie charged for the side of the barn, leading him straight past the structure and toward a house an eighth of a mile up the drive.

The Acker family home was everything he'd imagined, but nothing like he'd expected. Vaughn, New Mexico, wasn't exactly the type of place people from renovation shows visited. Not when a single man controlled the import and export of every grain of rice, wheat and piece of fruit. Jobs here consisted of farming the land, livestock raising and the occasional trade. The nearest dentist or physicians were in the next town over. Henry Acker and the townspeople didn't trust anyone outside these borders. More likely to take care of any ailments themselves and utilize natural remedies they'd made or stockpiled over the years. But the Acker home itself could've starred in one of those design shows.

Clean white horizontal siding gave the impression of a large home, but the structure couldn't have been more than two-thousand square feet. Dark shutters highlighted large windows from the covered porch. Old brick steps—handlaid from the looks of it—were still in perfect condition. As though the place had been built yesterday. An equally well-built redbrick chimney stretched up along one side of the house. Despite the constant threat the people of this town believed was coming, Henry Acker had done a fine job taking care of his home.

Understanding hit as Charlie hiked up the steps.

"You're not serious about going in there." Granger pulled up short. Zeus ran into his leg, unable to stop his mass quick enough. Happened more often than not. "Your father ordered us to leave. Not to mention anyone could be inside."

Charlie swung the screen door open. Old hinges screamed in protest, but it didn't stop her from shouldering inside the house. "If I followed every order my father gave me, Granger, I'd be buried next to my sisters' headstones in the backyard."

She didn't wait for his response, letting the house consume her.

Wind shifted through the trees protecting the property from the rest of the town with a false sense of privacy. Large thin trees that had no business growing here in the middle of the desert. Granger stared past the house, through the trees as an uncomfortable weight of being watched hitched his pulse higher. He didn't have a choice. Because a stranger standing outside Henry Acker's house was sure to attract attention. And not the good kind.

"Come on, Zeus." He and the bull terrier followed after Charlie up onto the porch, though Zeus had far more trouble than usual. Damn dog had probably gotten into something else he shouldn't have. Old boards creaked with his additional weight as a pair of rocking chairs—most likely hand hewn—shifted back and forth from the breeze. He had a perfect view of the driveway and the barn from this angle. Less chance of an ambush. Granger worked his way inside, instantly confronted with wood paneling, orange drapes and a wood-trimmed bay window looking out into the side yard. A thin layer of dust coated decades-old family photos, and cracked leather couches hinted at the stark difference between the outside of the home compared to the inside. Strong and pulled together on the exterior. Suffering on the inside. Granger catalogued everything within sight as he moved through the squared-off wood-trim arch into the kitchen. "Charlie?"

Old cabinetry stuck out. Old appliances. Wood countertops. A table with six chairs stood alone in the over-sized space of the kitchen. The dining room looked as though it hadn't gotten any use in years. No new scratches against the linoleum. What the hell were they doing here? What was Charlie hoping to find? A stack of boxes stuffed behind the dining table threatened to tip over at any second. Overpacked. Granger rounded the end of the table and pried the lid of the top box open as Zeus sniffed his way around the kitchen. Most likely looking for crumbs off the floor.

"It's meticulously inventoried." Charlie's voice had lost some of the power it'd had as they'd witnessed a man beaten to near death, and Granger couldn't help but take it in. The vulnerability, the pain that came with coming back here. She crossed the kitchen from the family room and pried the other lid open, pointing out the handwritten numbers on the underside of the cardboard. "Every week for the past twenty years. See these?"

She slid her finger closer to the beginning of the numbers where the handwriting had changed.

Granger pulled himself up taller, having not really come to terms that this place was where Charlie and her sisters had been raised. Until now. "Is that your handwriting?"

"One of my weekly jobs. I was in charge of inventorying all of our supplies. Here in the house and out back in the bunker. I had to make sure nothing was unaccounted for. Doesn't look like much has changed in that regard." She studied the kitchen as though seeing it for the first time.

"And if the numbers didn't match up?" He wasn't sure he wanted to know the answer, but these were the kinds of things he and Charlie had kept out of their short relationship. The stuff she hadn't wanted to give up to the man looking for a way to arrest her father. Not out of any kind of loyalty to Henry Acker but as a way to move on. To distance herself from the life she would be leaving behind.

"Then I would have to replace it with my own wages.

If it happened enough times, I paid for it in other ways, but when you're trying to escape an extremist group, you make sure that never happens." She folded the lids back into place, sealing the inventory inside. "You know, I was here last night, but it was so hard to see. In the daylight, it's almost like..."

Granger couldn't look away from the familiarity softening her face. It was nothing like that invisible armor she insisted on presenting to the world. Here, in her childhood home, she reminded him of the woman he'd known ten years ago. "Like what?"

"Like I'm home. I haven't felt that way in a long time." She shook her head, snapping herself back into the moment. "If my father catches us in here, his warning won't matter. He's very protective of his property. No one outside the family is allowed to even know this stuff exists."

She was right. They were running out of time. Acker's supplies, the house, her childhood—none of it had anything to do with her sister's death. "Did you find anything during your search?"

"I went through Erin's room again, but it's the same as last night." Charlie threaded her dark hair out of her face, highlighting the terra-cotta coloring of her skin. Henry Acker was the epitome of an angry white man determined to protect his constitutional rights in the extreme, but somewhere along the way he'd fallen for a woman of Cameroon heritage. Charlie had never told him about her mother. Another one of those pieces of her childhood she wanted to forget. "My father has an office at the end of the hall. He always kept it locked, even when I was a kid. Going in there was forbidden, and I wasn't masochist enough to break that rule. If there's something tying him to Erin's death or any of the attacks you suspect him of being involved in, it would be in there."

Granger crossed the kitchen to the window above the sink. Only this window didn't give him a visual on the barn or the front of the house. A cement bunker took up most of the view. It wouldn't take long before someone found the men they'd knocked unconscious. "We better move fast. The sun is behind the trees now. It'll be ten times harder to get out of town if we can't see where we're going."

"I've got that covered." Charlie didn't wait for him to catch up as she vanished back into the family room. Zeus took it upon himself to follow her. Traitor.

Granger tracked her past worn couches, an old box TV and a crocheted rug that'd seen better days. The house wasn't large, making it easy to navigate down the hallway where Charlie crouched in front of the last door in the hall. "Any idea where we're supposed to get a key?"

"I don't need one." The door fell open. Only as she stood did he recognize the miniature lockpick set she was sliding back into her jacket. Shoving to her feet, she smiled, with victory etched into her face.

"Another one of your weekly tasks when you were a kid?" he asked.

"No. That one I picked up on my own." She grabbed the doorknob and pushed inside the too-small office taken over by the massive desk in the center of the room. Charlie didn't wait for permission, rounding the other side of the desk. She tested drawers and went through papers as Granger surveyed the rest of the room.

A closet stood off to his right, pulling him toward it as effectively as gravity held him to the earth. He dragged the door open. And stepped back. Guns. Lots of guns. Granger lost count after he hit twenty, and that was just the rifles. Reaching for one dead center of the lineup, he tested the modifications. High-powered and definitely not used for hunting. At least not the legal kind. Boxes of ammunition stacked along the overhead shelf nearly reached the ceiling. "He's got enough guns here for an entire army."

Though he guessed that was the point.

"Granger." Charlie's voice had taken on that wispy quality again. "I found something."

He replaced the weapon on its mount and shut the closet door behind him. "What is it?"

She flattened what looked like a blueprint across the desk with both hands. "Plans."

"These are dated two weeks ago." Granger took out his phone and took a photo. Handwritten notes took up the margins, with lines cutting across the page. He sent the photo to Scarlett Beam, Socorro's security specialist. If anyone could get them an answer, it was her. "Looks like the layout of a building, but I won't know from where until I get one of my teammates to look at them."

"You don't need to. I already know where these blueprints are from, and I know what my father is up to." She took a step back, though she didn't take her attention off the blueprints in front of her. "He's planning to attack the state capital."

Chapter Five

This couldn't be right.

Her father and his homegrown army had never plotted something this big before. Age was supposed to come with wisdom. Where the hell was Henry Acker's common sense? Attacking a state capital building would put him behind bars for the rest of his life. However long he had left anyway.

Charlie grabbed for the blueprints, crumpling the thin paper between both hands. No. She wasn't going to let this happen. She'd find a way to stop him, even if it meant taking the few notes he'd made in the margins. Heavy footsteps echoed through the house from the porch. "We need to go."

"Leave the blueprints. I've got photos." Granger grabbed her arm and tried to maneuver her toward the door.

She tugged herself free, looking for anything else that might slow Acker's Army down. They were already responsible for so many lives. She couldn't let them do this. "We can't leave these here."

The front door screen protested, just as it had when she'd pulled it open to come inside.

Granger got close—too close—pressing his chest against her arm. His mouth dropped to her ear. "If you take them, he'll know we've been in here. He'll know we found them, and he might change his plans. Right now, we have a way to stop him, Charlie. Do you really want to risk that?"

He was right. Of course, he was right. But the thought of allowing her father to do what he did best knotted panic deep in her gut. The front door creaked open with two even thuds. Only her father wasn't coming inside the house. At least not completely.

Charlie nodded, forcing herself to release her hold on the blueprints. "There's a hatch that leads under the house on the left side of the closet."

Granger didn't hesitate. He released her, leaving a cold trail of sensation around her arm. Swinging the closet door open, he shoved her father's hunting camo hanging across the metal bar out of the way and exposed their only escape.

Sundown had passed.

They were out of time.

Charlie quieted her breathing to listen for signs of movement as Granger worked to clear the hatch. There was nothing to suggest her father suspected she hadn't left town as ordered, but the one mistake she'd made growing up was underestimating the monster he kept inside. The one he only let out when he was in the middle of one of his operations.

Her gaze cut back to the blueprints, then to Granger. She already lived with the guilt of four innocent lives taken that night at the Alamo pipeline, not including her oldest sister. She couldn't handle the weight of any more. She couldn't give Henry Acker the chance to even try. Charlie closed the distance between her and the desk for a second time and folded the main blueprint as quickly as possible. She shoved the plans down the back waistband of her jeans.

Granger hauled the hatch open and reached back for her. "You first."

Old wood whined from the hallway. Just outside the office door.

Air caught in her throat as she watched a shadow shift beneath the crack between the floor and the bottom of the door. Fear and a thousand questions bubbled up her throat. She needed to know why. Why her father had become an enemy of his own government. Why he'd decided the lives of the people of this town were worth sacrificing in a losing battle. Because no matter how many attacks Acker's Army carried out, they were going to lose. *He* was going to lose, and when that happened, everyone she'd ever loved would be gone.

"Charlie, we've got to go." Granger latched onto her hand and pulled her into the closet. He shoved her into the square opening and pressed her head down.

Cold air whipped her hair into her face. She kept low and moved fast as she headed for the back of the house. Zeus dropped out of the opening behind her with a huff.

A gunshot ripped through the wood flooring.

"Go!" Granger was out of the opening and shoving her forward.

Her nerves shot into overdrive. Charlie clawed out from underneath the house.

Another bullet exploded from behind them. "Charlie!" Her father's bellow seemed to shake the house right off its minimal foundation. "Get back here, girl!"

Granger's hand found hers as they ran for the trees. They kept pace with each other as though they'd been together this entire time. Like they'd never lost touch.

Twigs and pine needles scratched at her hair and face as they broke the line of trees that'd stood guard over her family's property her entire childhood. Once upon a time, she'd known these trees as well as she'd known the back of her own hand. Dozens of summers of her and her sisters playing hide-and-seek struggled to fit into the overgrowth and darkness. Despite the encroaching desert and miserable temperatures throughout most the year, this patch of paradise went on for miles. Her family had relied on it more than once for wood in the winter, for mushrooms in the spring and growing produce not meant to survive in this part of the world in the summer.

They'd made a mistake coming here.

Henry Acker never gave up, and he never surrendered. Even when faced with the exposed involvement and potential arrest of his daughters for his dirty deeds, he hadn't admitted anything that could implicate him in his attacks. And he wouldn't stop looking for her. Not after knowing she was the one to take his blueprints. There was a chance she and Granger would never make it out of Vaughn, and she'd lose the one tie to that old life she'd never wanted to let go of. Him.

Her breathing overwhelmed the pounding of her footsteps until it was all she could hear. She'd been running for so long she wasn't sure she could stop. Her body wouldn't let her. Not until she got them as far from this place as possible. It was the only way to survive what was coming for them.

"Charlie." Granger grabbed for her, but she wouldn't slow down. She couldn't. "He's not following us. You can stop." His hand latched around hers, and he seemed to anchor her to the spot. Her momentum swung her into that comforting wall of muscle, but the need to keep fighting was too strong. Arms of steel secured her against his frame. "Charlie, stop."

She couldn't contain the sobs. They cut through her like thousands of shards of glass. "He's coming for us. He's never going to let me go. No matter how hard I fight or how long I hide, I'll never escape this place. I'll never escape him."

"I've got you." His hand threaded through her hair as something warm and slobbery collapsed against her leg. The dog. "I gave you my word when you agreed to be my CI. I'm not going to let him touch you. Ever. Understand?"

She latched onto that promise with everything she had as the adrenaline rush of escape ran out. Because it was the only thing that made sense in this world. The internal battle between loving the man who'd raised her and the man who'd carelessly sacrificed innocent lives for his cause—including her sisters'—was tearing her apart, piece by piece. But Granger was holding her together right now. And that was enough.

Charlie brought her arms around him, taking in everything she could about these few seconds. They'd had moments like this that'd sustained her before her disappearance, but this…this felt different. Stronger and more fragile at the same time. It was familiar and terrifying and absolutely needed in the middle of a fight for their lives. "My father will already have someone raiding your vehicle for supplies. We're stuck out here without flashlights or a compass or a plan. Sooner or later, he's going to send someone in to flush us out. For this."

She pulled the blueprints from the back of her waistband. Sweat permeated the paper. There was a chance she'd screwed this up. But letting Henry Acker go through with his plans and potentially being too late to stop him wasn't a risk she'd been willing to take.

"You took the blueprints." No hint of disappointment. Nothing to suggest anger or any other emotion got the better of him. And hell, she wished Granger would show her something. That she could read him as well as she used to. "No wonder your father's pissed."

"I just wanted…" The pain of that night, of watching people die because she'd been too weak to stand up to her father, clawed through her. "I wanted to do something good for once. Something that might make up for my mistakes. I can't let him hurt anyone else, Granger."

"It's going to be okay. We'll figure this out. Together." Granger secured her against him. Right where she needed to be. "Not sure if you know this, but I have a little experience with getting out of tough situations."

The rumble of his voice soothed her cracked nerves, and Charlie wanted nothing more than to stay in this moment for a little longer. To pretend her father wasn't about to attack the state's most protected landmark. That ten years of silence hadn't changed things between her and Granger.

But they had.

She pulled out of his arms. Because no matter how much she wanted to believe they were the same people they'd been back then, it just wasn't true. Her fingers grazed the left side of his rib cage. Wetness spread across her fingertips. Concern hijacked her central nervous system. "You're hit."

"It's nothing." Granger clamped a hand over the wound, coming away with blood in the last blur of sundown. He cut his attention down to hide the flash of pain in his expression. "Just a graze. It'll stop bleeding as long as I keep pressure on it."

"You were shot. That's not nothing." Charlie shoved the blueprints back into her waistband and ripped her jacket from her shoulders in a flurry of needing to do something. "Take off your shirt. I need to see the wound."

"It's fine. I've survived worse. We need to get moving if we want to stay ahead of your dad's underlings." He attempted a step forward, but Charlie wouldn't let him budge.

She planted a hand on his chest, directly over that heart she'd once believed belonged to her. That was the thing about fairy tales. They'd always been too good to be true. Including the one she'd created between them. "Unless you're trained in field medicine like I am, you're going to do exactly as I tell you. Now sit down and lift up your shirt."

SHE WAS GOING to be the death of him.

And not in any kind of physical way.

Granger braced against the boulder jutting out from a grouping a trees. A place like these woods shouldn't exist in the middle of the New Mexico desert, but the people of Vaughn had taken advantage of the protection they offered between them and the outside world.

He took out his phone, raising it up to search for those out-of-reach bars. No service. No way to get ahold of Socorro out here. The photo he'd sent to Scarlett with those blueprints hadn't gone through. Hell, Henry Acker and his army were probably dismantling his satellite phone from the SUV at this very moment. Preppers didn't like to rely on government-monitored technology. Too many chances they'd attract attention or tip their hands. In fact, he knew firsthand that Henry Acker forbid the use of any kind of cell phone within Vaughn. They mostly worked with private radio channels if they had to communicate. Wouldn't do Granger or Charlie a bit of good out here though.

Zeus stared at him from a few feet away with those marble-like black eyes, ready to pounce on Granger's command. But despite the image of Charlie struggling to get out from under the bull terrier again, his wound was still bleeding. Adding pressure hadn't done a damn thing the past few minutes. Which meant the graze was worse than he'd originally estimated. She was right. They were stuck out here in the middle of a hostile town without supplies, first aid or an idea of where to run.

"Hold still. I need to get a look at the wound." The sound of something tearing reached his ears. The skin across his stomach tightened in response to the outside elements filtering through the lost fabric of his shirt. Every muscle in his torso tensed at her touch, and Granger couldn't help but flinch at the contact. "Sorry. Cold hands."

"Don't apologize. Just do what you have to do." Every second they wasted trying to get his wound taken care of was another second Henry Acker had to find them. Oxygen sucked through his teeth as he tried to relax against her probing. Pain spiked through him and bucked his shoulders against the boulder. "Except that. Don't do that again."

"You're right. It's a graze, but it's pretty deep." She sat back on her heels, searching for something around them. Hauling herself upright, she collected something out of sight. "This might sting at first, but the longer we leave it pressed against the wound, the faster it'll stop bleeding."

Hell, he'd taken a bullet through his shoulder less than three weeks ago. A graze should be nothing. But it was as though his senses and pain receptors had gone into overdrive with Charlie so close. Enough for him to recognize the plant in her hand. "Is that a cactus?"

"Prickly pear. The pads contain astringent and antiseptic qualities. I've had to use them a couple times growing up around here. Lucky for you, we're surrounded by them. And if this doesn't work, we can use pine sap. Same antiseptic properties, just harder to get to." Unholstering a small blade from an ankle holster he hadn't spotted until now, she set to work stripping the cactus of its thick skin as easily as an apple. "Figured you Socorro types would be required to carry your own first-aid kits with the kind of work you do."

"We are." He watched her hands move as though she'd done this a thousand times before. Which she most likely had, growing up in a place that put so much value on independence and using what one had to survive. "Mine is in the SUV."

Her laugh rolled between them. She flipped the blade of her knife closed and holstered the small weapon, shuffling forward on her knees to get closer. Charlie had removed the hot pink bulbs on the edges of the cactus and stripped the skin down until nothing but a shiny surface remained. Maneuvering what was left of his shirt out of the way, she pressed the cool flesh of the plant against his rib cage. Instant relief melted across his skin and took the pain of the wound. "Well, thank goodness I'm here. Otherwise you might have to use that dog to get you out of this mess, and we all know he's going to get distracted by whatever food he comes across."

"Hey. Zeus is perfectly capable of staying on task when ordered," he said. "It's all the other times I have to make sure he doesn't accidentally eat my mattress or shoes."

"Here. Hold this in place while I make some bandages." She grabbed for his hand and used it to secure the cactus to his side. Charlie collected her knife once again and set about cutting through the jacket she'd been wearing, shaping them into long strips. "How long have you been together? You and Zeus?"

"Going on nine years." Granger mentally double-checked his math as Zeus pushed his front paws into the dirt and settled down. Apparently, the bull terrier had realized Charlie wasn't going anywhere. "Came into my life right when I needed him and hasn't left since. Though I'm not sure he could at this point. Any other K9 unit would've shipped him off to the shelter for his binge-eating."

"I've never met a dog with an eating disorder." Charlie measured out the longest stretch of denim from her jacket and wound it around his rib cage. Her mouth came into contact with his ear, and a shiver of warmth exploded through him. Too soon, she pulled back to secure the cactus in place. "And wow. Nine years? And all that time was with Socorro?"

Granger forced himself to take a breath that wasn't coated in Charlie's scent. Soap with a bite of citrus. "Ivy recruited me after I left Homeland. Every operative is assigned a dog when we sign on with Socorro, but we all know the K9s are the real heroes. They detect explosives, identify remains, protect our handlers against threats. They have our backs when we're in danger of taking our eyes off the mission. Loyal to the end."

"And what does Zeus do other than suffocate people with his enormous weight?" Her fingers worked to straighten the bandages, though they didn't need to be straight to do their job, and a piece of him realized it'd been years since Charlie had let herself connect with someone else like this. It was human nature to want affection and to give that attention to someone else. And she'd denied herself since the moment she'd run.

Zeus snapped his head to attention at the mention of his name, then slowly army-crawled closer until he was able to set his chin over Granger's leg.

"This chunk is the best tracker the Pentagon has.

Once he picks up a scent, he doesn't let it go until he finds its location." Granger scrubbed his hand between the K9's ears. "I think that's one of the reasons he's been able to get into my stash of treats at the top of my closet. He never gives up."

"You two seem close." Charlie let her hands fall back into her lap. She'd taken care of his wound and ensured he wouldn't bleed out before they came up with a plan to get the hell out of here. He owed her for that. "You're different now. The counterterrorism agent I knew would've spent the rest of his life hunting down terrorists for Homeland Security. Not playing house with an overweight dog."

Granger pressed back into the boulder to get his legs underneath him. A deep ache wrapped around his rib cage, but it was nothing compared to the initial pain. The cactus was doing its job. He just hoped it'd keep him on his feet.

"Yeah, well, I didn't exactly have a choice." He inventoried the supplies and weapons on his person. Not much. And not nearly enough if they ran into trouble. The sun had disappeared completely behind the mountains. His vision would adjust to the darkness, but they still had to figure a way out of Vaughn without coming across Acker's path. "After that night at the Alamo pipeline, I had to come clean about my source. My superiors weren't too thrilled I'd taken on a member of Acker's Army as my CI. Not to mention the fact that I'd gotten her killed. Every piece of intel I'd gathered on your father and his army was questioned and discarded, especially since I had no way of proving any of it was real.

Seems the United States government wasn't willing to risk keeping me around."

Charlie got to her feet. "You were fired? Because of me? Even though you knew I hadn't died in that explosion."

"Yeah. I knew." He took another step. To add some distance between them. To make sense of what they'd gotten themselves into. Charlie had taken her father's blueprints, and right now, they had no way of getting that information to his team without cell service. But the part of him that had believed she'd died in the attack on the pipeline that night didn't want the distance. It wanted nothing more than to protect her like he should have that night. "Didn't make a damn bit of difference though. You'd gone off the grid. And I realized after a few months you weren't coming back. In the end, it was for the best. I moved on, landed this job with Socorro. With Homeland, I was always too late. Always at the scene of an attack after it'd already happened, but now I have a chance to stop attacks before they happen. I can save lives before they're ruined."

"Granger, I—"

Static cut through the trees.

Granger rounded on her and slid his hand over her mouth. Her exhale warmed his hand as they waited for a sign they weren't alone.

There. North of their position. The static was louder now. Getting closer. He removed his hand, angling down for his sidearm. He whispered in Charlie's ear. "Behind me. Move."

She did as he asked.

But her impulsive move to redistribute her weight snapped a dry twig—too loud in the silence.

"Over here!" An explosion of brightness overwhelmed Granger's senses as a flare shot straight into the air.

They'd been found.

"Run. Now!" He shoved Charlie ahead of him as multiple shouts followed them through the pines. The enemy would cut them off if Granger gave them the chance. He wasn't going to let that happen. Zeus's growl registered as the K9 struggled to keep up. Granger dropped back and hauled the dog over his shoulder. Pain ripped through his side from the bullet graze, but he'd have to rely on adrenaline to get him through. "Keep going."

A second flare lit up their position. Only this one had been shot horizontally. It hit a tree ten feet in front of them and exploded on impact.

Granger grabbed for her. "Charlie!"

She protected her face as the tree burst into flames, falling back to counter her momentum. Granger rushed to keep her from losing her balance, but it was too late. He, Zeus and Charlie all hit the ground as one.

The flames jumped from the originating tree to the next and the next.

Blistering heat cut them off from escape as a wall of darkness and flames moved in.

Chapter Six

Pain seared up her back and into the base of her skull.

"Get her to the truck. He'll want to deal with her himself," a voice said. "Leave the agent and the dog. Let the flames have the bodies."

A glow penetrated the seam of her eyelids. Too bright. Too hot. Charlie fought to shake off the haze clouding her head. She was moving. Not being carried. Dragged. Gravel and rock cut through her thin T-shirt, her arms stretched above her head. The voice was too low to put a face to. Him. Who was *him*? Her father?

She wasn't going back to her father. She wouldn't help him in another attack. No matter what he threatened her with this time.

Movement registered in her mind, growing more distant.

Charlie forced herself to come around, struggling to escape that addictive pull of unconsciousness. Heat burned along one side of her body. Blistering enough to kick her brain into gear. *Kill the agent.*

Panic swelled in her throat as her mind processed the meaning of each of those words. They'd escaped her father's house. Granger had been grazed by a bullet.

She'd treated the wound as best she could and secured it with her jacket. And then…they were running. A flash of red shot across her mind. The flare gun. Someone had shot at them with a flare gun. "Granger."

"Tranquila," that voice said. Quiet.

Grabbing for a half-buried rock, she tried to wrench herself out of the man's hold, but it was no use. He was too strong and had too much leverage. She secured her hand around the base of the next tree and kicked with everything she had.

Her boot slipped free in her abductor's hand. He turned on her, his features aglow in the flames spreading fast through the woods. Charlie rolled out of reach and dodged his attempt. She grabbed for her ankle holster, coming up empty.

"Looking for this?" The clarity of her attacker's features diminished with the appearance of her knife in his hand. He tossed her boot out of sight. "There's nowhere for you to run, *chica*. No one escapes *Sangre por Sangre*."

Sangre por Sangre? The cartel? Understanding hit. These men didn't work for her father. The cartel Granger and Socorro had warned her about had finally found her. How?

Smoke burned down the back of her throat. The heat intensified, beading sweat along her hairline. The fire was consuming everything in its path. And sooner or later, it would consume her and everyone left in these trees. Charlie turned her attention on a way out, but the man holding her at knifepoint was blocking the only escape. She would have to go through him. "What the hell do you people want from me?"

"To restore *Sangre por Sangre* to its original glory," he said.

Charlie dared a step back. Her heel landed on a smoldering branch. The wood cracked and sent embers around her legs. "I'm not doing anything for you or the people you work for. Understand?"

A low laugh crackled over the flames. "Not even when your father's life depends on it?"

"What are you talking about?" A thread of cold worked through her. "How do you know my father? And where is Granger?"

"We know everything about you, Charlie Acker." The man with her knife stepped to his left, forcing her to counter as he attempted to circle behind her. He was giving her an opportunity to run. Almost as though he was daring her to take the risk, to give him the chance to hunt her down. The steel of her blade glimmered in the reflection of flames. He was all that was standing between her and freedom from this place. "The work you did for your father. Where you've been hiding all these years. Did you really think my superiors fell for your ruse?"

He tsked, shaking his head. "You planned the attack on the Alamo pipeline. It was you who put Acker's Army on the map. Not your father. And now, you're going to do the same for us."

The need for answers battled with her survival instincts until paralysis held her in place. The fire would be seen for miles. Vaughn didn't have a large fire department, but the people of this town were prepared for any disaster, natural or not. Someone was coming. Charlie spotted a downed, rotted-out branch between her and the only escape. "Did your cartel kill my sister?"

"You're wasting time," he asked. "Pretty soon neither of us will be able to walk out of here alive."

"Then I suggest you answer the question." The sweat was almost suffocating now, prickling along both sides of her face, but the worst was at her back, where the blueprints poked into her skin. "Did the cartel have her killed? When *Sangre por Sangre* couldn't get to me, did they kill her and leave her to rot in these woods to draw me out?"

"Come with me without a fight, and I'll tell you everything you want to know about your sister's death." The promise hung between them for two seconds. Three. Her attacker closed the blade in his hand, offering it to her. It would be so tempting to believe she could just reach out and take it. That she could escape, but Charlie had learned to recognize false promises long before the cartel had come into her life. He was trying to establish a rapport, trying to take the fight out of her. He wasn't going to give her any information. Instead, he and the people he worked for would dangle that carrot and the lives of everyone she cared about in front of her until they forced her to do what they wanted. Because that was how power worked. "Or...start running. It's been a long time since I've had a challenge, but I can't promise how our game will end."

Charlie had been controlled enough in her life.

"That's it? I come with you willingly, you leave my

family alone and you tell me what happened to my sister?" She took a step forward as though to accept his offer, one hand stretched out.

"That's it." That voice eased through her. Trusting, confident.

"Why don't I believe you?" Charlie lunged for the downed branch at her feet and swung as hard as she could. The tip of the rotted wood slammed against her abductor's head, and he shot off to one side. Her blade hit the ground in a burst of embers. She grabbed for it, burning her hand on the growing flames, and ran.

His scream bellowed behind her as she raced for the only clearing of trees not on fire.

"Get her!" Anger replaced the trust and confidence in her attacker's words, and Charlie pumped her legs faster.

Her pulse skyrocketed with the added pressure on her lungs to keep up, but she couldn't stop. Not until she found Granger and Zeus. Shouts bled through the trees around her. There were four of them. Maybe five. All closing in on her position.

Shadows shifted up ahead, and Charlie darted to the left to avoid contact. She had no idea where she was. No idea where the cartel would take Granger and Zeus. A tremor vibrated through her legs the harder she pushed. She was running on empty and most likely suffering from a concussion, but experience told her all those punishing laps she'd run around the farm would keep her on her feet for hours if necessary.

Charlie heard the snap of wood behind her.

A force she'd only ever encountered in the aftermath of the Alamo pipeline explosion slammed into her. She hit the ground face first. Air crushed from her chest as the weight on her back increased.

"I told you. No one escapes *Sangre por Sangre*." Her attacker dug his knee into her back to make a point.

Flashes of memory—of being pinned beneath a man twice her size and struggling to breathe—forced their way to the front of her mind. A training exercise. One in which she'd lost consciousness as rain pounded on her back. Her father's face in the center of her vision. Only she wasn't twelve years old anymore.

The glow of flames grew brighter. Ash collected around her face. Sweat collected on her upper lip. She could hear the roar of the fire drawing near. This was her last chance.

Charlie threw her elbow back as hard as she could. Bone connected with her attacker's shin, taking away his leverage as his knee flared in the same direction as her momentum. She rolled hard and fast. One kick to his groin. That was all it took to bring him down. He landed face-first as she crawled to her feet. Her lungs had yet to get the message to inhale, but she couldn't wait.

She darted for a tree big enough to hide her.

Just as a bullet punctured the bark.

"You won't make it, Charlie!" The cartel soldier had lost that smooth manipulation in his voice. Instead, a demon seemed to be trying to tear free from his chest. "You're in too deep now."

Pressing her skull into the bark, Charlie finally caught her breath. He was right. She wouldn't make it as long as she'd brought a knife to a gunfight. She closed her eyes to calm her fight-or-flight instincts. She had to think.

She'd grown up on this land. Knew more about it than anyone else. There had to be something here…

The shed. The one she would run to when training, or dealing with two sisters, or losing her father's approval hit a little too hard. It was nothing compared to what she kept on hand in the safe houses she'd built over the years, but there were supplies. Weapons. She just had to remember where it was. And hope her father hadn't demolished and raided it.

Footsteps cut through the chaos in her head.

Charlie scanned the trees up ahead. They were thinner. If she ran, she'd lose her cover. But it was worth it.

"There's nowhere to run." His voice had regained some of that control she'd noted earlier. "Whether you like it or not, you belong to *Sangre por Sangre* now, Charlie. You are going to change everything for us."

She picked a spot through two pine trees ahead. And ran.

The second bullet whizzed past her by a couple of feet.

But the third hit its mark.

ZEUS'S BARK PUNCTURED through the haze of unconsciousness.

Granger tried to get past the roll of nausea in his gut, but he lost the battle. Turning onto his side, he emptied his stomach as the bull terrier tugged on the cuff of his pants. The K9's whine was nothing compared to the heat blistering along Granger's back. "I'm up. I'm up."

He planted both hands on the ground and shoved to stand. Facing off with a ring of fire closing in. "Oh, hell."

Zeus backed into Granger's leg.

There was no escape. Every tree around them had caught fire, and they had nowhere to go. The flames inched forward every second Granger tried to come up with a plan, but they were out of options. Acid lingered in his throat. The wind kicked up, aggravating the wall of heat. Tendrils danced and flickered toward them. He collected Zeus from the ground as embers flared at their feet. The K9's added weight pulled on the wound along his ribs. "It's going to be okay, buddy. We've been through worse."

A crack of wood pierced through the raging fire growing louder. A tree off to their right groaned a split second before Granger caught sight of the top tipping toward them. "Hang on, Zeus!"

He lunged out of the way. They hit the ground with a hard thud. Granger's shoulder screamed as the shard of bullet left inside took the impact. Rolling onto his back, he could barely make out the stars through the thickness of the smoke. An ember burned through the sleeve of his shirt and down to skin. Searing pain kept him in the moment when all his brain wanted to do was give up. Granger swatted at the ember as Zeus climbed to his feet. "We got to get out of here."

Reaching for Zeus, he hit the emergency tracking built into the K9's collar. He didn't know if the signal would go through without cell service, but he had to try. It would take the Socorro team at least an hour to arrive on site. Granger just hoped to hell and back there was something left here for them to save. Sweat dripped into his eyes as he maneuvered onto all fours. The ring of flames was closing in fast, giving them less than eight feet in circumference to work with. And they were the only ones inside. "Charlie."

Granger scoured the base of the flames around them. Looking for a sign of something that would tell him she'd gotten out of this alive, but it was too hard to determine with the wind aggravating the fire. No. She had to be alive. Nothing else mattered. "Charlie!"

Zeus called after her with a low howl.

No answer.

"We can do this, boy." Tearing through the knotted denim Charlie had tied around his ribs to hold the raw cactus against his wound, Granger secured the denim over his mouth and nose and tied another knot at the back of his head. A single layer wouldn't do much, but it was better than nothing, as the oxygen decreased this close to the ground.

Granger searched his holster. Empty. The men who'd attacked them with the flare gun must've taken his firearm. Damn it. They were going to pay for that. If they ever got out of this alive. He searched for something—anything—that could be used as a weapon. Every second he wasted wondering if Charlie was alive was another second he was stealing from himself and Zeus. If he didn't get out of here, there wasn't anything he could do to keep her out of the wrong hands. He'd already failed her once. He wasn't going to lose her again.

Another gust of wind drove the fire into the protective circle around them.

Whatever he was going to do, he had to do it now.

"Where is she, Zeus?" Granger ripped the denim off

his face and positioned it under the K9's nose. The dog buried his dry nose in the fabric as his tail went wild. He had the scent. A low gruff said Zeus knew exactly where Charlie had gone. Or where she'd been taken. The bull terrier lunged across the circle, kept inside by a wall of fire. "Good boy."

Granger kicked a four-inch dead pine branch free of its trunk. It wasn't much, but it could get the job done as long as he used it well. Closing the distance between him and the spot Zeus had alerted to, he faced off with the flames. He pushed the K9 behind him in case a rogue flame lashed out. Zeus was the only one who could find Charlie. Granger was going to do whatever it took to make that happen. Firemen trained for moments like this in full gear and armed with containers of oxygen. He didn't even have gloves. Still, this had to work. "This is going to hurt, but we've got no other choice."

He hauled the makeshift weapon overhead. Then slammed it down on the tree slowly burning to ashes. The branch he hit fell to the ground, taking the flames consuming it with it. He did it again, then again, breaking the tree to pieces. Embers lit up with each strike and attached to his skin and clothing, but he couldn't stop. He was almost through. He just needed another foot to get through the wall of heat.

A whisper of warning sizzled up his spine.

Granger turned just in time to watch as the ground he'd once stood on caught fire. Grabbing for Zeus, he pulled the K9 through the too-small opening he'd made by taking down one of the burning trees.

Just as the circle closed.

The dog was shaking in his arms, and Granger had no assurances he'd done anything to extend their lives. Because the fight wasn't over. They'd made it out of a small section of woods, but this entire place was on fire. Granger set his forehead against the dog's shoulder. "Take me to Charlie, Zeus, and let's get the hell out of here."

The bull terrier locked onto the same direction he'd indicated a few minutes ago and bolted ahead as far as the next obstacle in their way. A headache pulsed at the back of Granger's head with every swing of the branch to clear their path. Pain radiated up his arms. Dehydration was setting in. Not to mention the blow to the head he'd taken earlier. But he couldn't stop. Not yet. Not until they located Charlie.

Granger pushed through pain and exhaustion, and memories of that night at the Alamo pipeline refused to let go. He'd tried to get to Charlie then too. Studying every body the coroner had bagged before he'd gotten onto the scene. Searching for some clue that his grief was lying to him. The fires had raged much like this one with the combination of pure oil and explosives. Even from beyond the perimeter the fire department had set, it'd been so hot; he could still feel the warmth on his face.

She'd lost faith in him. He knew that now. Despite everything they'd been through and the intel she'd stolen from inside Acker's Army, Charlie had felt like she'd had no other choice than to run. Not just from her father. From him. He'd put her in an impossible situation as a confidential informant: against the family who protected and raised her. And he hadn't been there for her.

Granger wouldn't make that mistake again. Pooling a

decade's worth of loss and shame into his next swing, he took down the tree in front of him. All her life, Charlie had been used—by her father, by Homeland Security, by him. Considered nothing but a tool rather than the strong, charismatic woman she was. Something to be discarded when she outlived her use. But she deserved to have someone in her life that fought for her. Just once. And he wanted to be that someone. "I'm coming for you, Charlie. No matter what it costs me."

Zeus charged through an opening ahead, out of sight.

"Damn it, dog. Wait for me!" Granger struggled to keep up.

A yip cut through the pound of his heart beating between his ears. Granger went on alert as he shoved through a barrier of trees the fire hadn't burned through. Smoke blunted his vision, and he tightened his grip on the branch. "Zeus?"

The K9 didn't respond.

He whistled in a tone only he and Zeus understood. And waited.

There wasn't a single time in Zeus's training that dog hadn't answered his call to heel. The glow of fire intensified behind him but barely cut through the haze of smoke ahead. Granger took a careful step—slow, calculated—as he relied on his senses.

Too late.

A glint of metal caught his attention.

Just before the blade of an axe sliced in front of his face.

Granger countered by throwing his weight to one side. Saving himself from losing a limb.

A growl escaped his attacker as the oversized frame of Henry Acker spun toward him. Something feral and dangerous bled from the man's eyes. The patriarch had lost all sense of age as he rushed Granger, axe at the ready.

Granger countered the onslaught. His back hit the tree behind him.

Charlie's father embedded the blade of the weapon into the bark of the tree beside Granger's head, then clamped a strong hand around Granger's throat. "I told you to leave, Morais. I warned you two to leave when you had the chance. So where is she? Where is Charlie?"

Latching onto the old man's wrist, Granger could've sworn his feet were coming off the ground. Given his size, weight and combat experience, it shouldn't have been possible. But this wasn't the same man who'd warned Charlie to leave town. This was the general of the most dangerous army in the country: one that'd taken its time shoring up its resources and didn't answer to the US government. The man was running on pure adrenaline. Granger struggled to breathe around the grip on his throat. Two more of Acker's soldiers left the safety of the trees, weapons aimed at Granger. "Shouldn't you... be asking your men who attacked...us?"

Henry Acker pressed his weight into the palm against Granger's throat with far more strength than should've been possible. "I never issued an attack order. My men are fighting to put out this fire."

Granger didn't have time for this. He slammed the base of his palm into Acker's inner elbow. The old man might've studied combat techniques, but there was no way in hell that experience matched Granger's govern-ment or private contractor training.

Acker's arm folded. Granger twisted his wrist one-hundred-and-eighty degrees and locked out the man's elbow, forcing Acker to his knees. All in the span of three seconds. The homegrown military general kept his scream to himself. Impressive. "I have a bullet graze on my ribs that says different, Acker."

Both of Acker's Army soldiers moved in to protect their leader.

Granger turned Acker to face them, using the old man as a shield in case this went south. "You shoot, and you'll only be killing him. Understand? Now where the hell is my dog?"

"You won't get away with this, Morais. She was safe, and you dragged her back. For what? To get to me? Something happens to her, I'll kill you," Henry Acker said. "I give you my word."

"You knew she was alive," Granger said. "How?"

Two gunshots echoed through trees over the roar on encroaching flames.

Granger loosened his hold on Henry Acker. *"Charlie."*

Chapter Seven

The bullet ripped across the side of her calf.

Charlie hit the ground short of the next cover of trees. Pain seared through her leg until she wasn't sure she'd be able to take her next breath. It was too much. Almost debilitating. But the thought of giving in to a cartel's demands when she'd fought to escape a life of control and punishment was stronger.

She dug her fingernails into the dirt ahead of her and pulled. Physical strength was a necessity of being a soldier of Acker's Army. No matter the situation, her father wouldn't have accepted anything less than her best at all times. Her training had started when she'd just been five years old, and it hadn't let up until she'd run the night of the pipeline explosion. Years of drills and weights gave her the strength to army crawl from her attacker as he advanced.

Only she wasn't fast enough.

A foot pressed down on her wound.

The resulting scream exploded through the trees and echoed back to her. Loud enough to scrub the back of her throat raw. White lights lit up behind her eyelids, brighter than the fire burning ever closer.

"I'm beginning to think you are unappreciative of my offer, though I do appreciate the challenge you've presented me tonight." That same smoky voice that had tried to convince her to trust him was back. Edging underneath her armor, chasing back the pain in her leg. "Just for that, I'll personally make sure your father suffers before I kill him."

"Touch him, and it will be the last thing you ever do." The words hissed through clenched teeth as she fed into an anger she hadn't let herself fall victim to in a long time. Because there was a difference between Henry Acker serving a prison sentence for the lives he'd destroyed through his attacks on government property and someone killing him to punish her. "I give you my word, and if you know anything about me and the way I was raised, you know I mean that."

His laugh attempted to disregard her threat as nothing more than a temper tantrum. The weight of his foot disappeared. Strong hands wrenched her arm behind her, forcing her to turn onto her back if she didn't want to dislocate her shoulder. He stared down at her, his features clearer now that she'd gotten some distance from the fire. Sharp ears stood out from a pristine haircut that fanned over his forehead. Sweat had glued his dark hair around his temples and hairline, but it was his eyes she paid attention to. Softer than expected. Lighter too. A thin layer of facial hair spread from his sideburns down along his jaw, giving him a younger appearance. This wasn't a hardened soldier of a drug cartel, and yet he carried himself and spoke with far more authority than the soldiers in her father's army would dare. "You have no idea who you're dealing with, do you? Who I am or what I've done to people standing in the way of what I want?"

Charlie brought her head off the ground in an attempt to make her point clear. "All I know is, right now, *you* are the man standing in my way."

Bullet be damned, she brought both legs up and wrapped them around his waist. In a move her father would be proud to see, Charlie hauled her attacker off to one side. She slammed his body into the ground and rolled on top of him. Adrenaline gave her a burst of fight as she rocketed her fist into his face. Once. Twice.

Blood spattered as bone crunched beneath her knuckles. His head snapped back, but not hard enough to knock him unconscious. Her attacker caught her third strike and twisted her arm in the wrong direction.

Her holler filled the trees around them, and she was forced to follow the arc of her arm. Charlie hit the ground, but she wouldn't let him get the upper hand. She rolled with everything she had as he struggled to pin her down. Dirt and ash drove into her mouth with every breath. Her leg screamed in protest, but she couldn't stop fighting. She shoved to all fours and tested her weight on her injured leg.

A third bullet pulverized the tree bark to her left. Her nerves shot into overdrive. Charlie froze, her hands over her head as though they could do anything to stop a bullet from killing her. There was no cover to hide behind. Nowhere she could run this time.

"My plan was to let you walk out of here on your own with me, Charlie, but it's not your legs I'm interested in. I just need that beautiful mind of yours, and my patience is wearing thin." Her attacker shifted his aim from the tree. To her. "I've given you plenty of chances to come to your senses, and I'm done playing nice. Now stand. We have work to do."

"You're making a mistake." Adrenaline drained from her veins—faster than she expected. She felt its loss as though the earth's gravity had somehow intensified over the past minute. Charlie braced herself against the tree at her back. There was no way for her to hold her own weight. No way she was getting out of this on her own. She pulled out the knife she'd taken back from him and flipped the blade open. The one her father had given her on her twelfth birthday after she's won a fight against four boys her age. It'd been a training test. To prove she could overcome, and it'd gotten her to this point. A blade this size wouldn't stop a bullet, but it would keep her going. Keep her fighting. Because she deserved the life she'd created for herself, and no one—not even a drug cartel—was going to take that away from her. "Whatever you want from me, whatever you think you can force me to do for your organization…it won't work. I've spent my entire life being told what to do, and I'm stronger than you think I am."

A bark preceded the charge of the overweight bull terrier.

The gunman's attention cut to the K9 lunging at him from the right.

And Charlie had her chance. "Zeus!"

She summoned what was left of her adrenaline and shoved to her feet. Zeus bit into the cartel soldier's forearm and pulled the son of a bitch down. His body and his gun hit the ground as his scream exploded through the clearing. Charlie dove for the weapon.

He knocked it out of her reach as he fought off the dog with a bellow that outmatched hers. The gun disappeared into the bushes. Out of sight. Blood seeped from the wound in her leg. Unstoppable and pounding.

Her attacker unholstered his own blade, arching it down toward the determined bull terrier.

"No!" She didn't have any other choice. Charlie wrenched his arm back, trying to get a hold of the weapon. The blade sliced into her palm, but she didn't have the sense to get clear. Not as long as Granger's partner was in danger. "Zeus!"

The K9 released his target. The sense of relief flooding through her was short lived as a fist slammed into her face.

The momentum and pain knocked her backward. Her leg threatened to collapse right out from underneath her. She fisted both hands together and brought them down on the soldier's arm. Swiping her own blade toward his chest, she overcorrected as he dodged her attempt. Charlie made up for her imbalance and aimed for his gut.

He caught her hand an inch from the tip of her blade meeting the soft tissue of his stomach. Then slammed his head into her face. A strong right hook followed and threw her off balance. Images of that fight—of her facing off with four boys her age—threatened to superimpose on her current reality. She'd taken more than her share of strikes, but this…this was different. Back then, her father would've stepped in if things had gone too far. Now she was on her own. And she was losing.

Charlie's leg failed, and she dropped to her knees, her back to her attacker. He moved in, but she wasn't finished. Locking her arm, she rotated with the blade aimed backward. Only it didn't reach its target.

Gripping her arm, the cartel soldier stared down at her. Just before rocketing his knuckles into her cheekbone. "I didn't want to do this, but now you leave me no other choice."

She lost her balance and hit the dirt. Zeus's whine echoed through her head, as though the dog actually cared about what happened next. The crackle of flames grew louder in her ears. Growing closer. They'd outrun the brunt of the fire, but it was always meant to catch up to them. To her. Charlie gripped onto the only thing she had left of that old life.

And stabbed it into the soldier's foot.

He threw his fist into her side and knocked the air out of her lungs.

Charlie collapsed. Desperation told her to keep moving. She climbed to her feet, dizzy from blood loss and swiped at him again. Another strike took the last of her energy reserves, and she went down again. She couldn't breathe, couldn't think.

The fight slipped out of her as she stared up into the smoke-darkened sky.

Her attacker spit blood and saliva at her feet. Bending to meet her, he fisted the collar of her shirt and started pulling. Her remaining boot caught against rock and dead pine needles. "I have to admit, I didn't expect so much fight from you, Charlie. Maybe if your sister fought as hard as you, she wouldn't be dead."

Charlie reached for her abductor's hand, trying to get free, but she wasn't strong enough anymore. Maybe hadn't been in a long time. Zeus whimpered as he watched. His bark shook through her, but worse was the battle she saw in his eyes, as determination to go against his command took hold. "No."

"Don't worry, Charlie. This will all be over soon," her attacker said. "You and I are going to do great things together. You'll see."

"ZEUS!" WHERE THE hell was that dog?

"You expect me to rely on a mutt who can't control his weight to find my daughter?" Henry Acker had called a temporary truce at the sound of those gunshots, but Granger didn't trust a single word out of the man's mouth. "What kind of agent are you anyway?"

They jogged to stay ahead of the fire while Acker's men worked to put it out from the other side, but the wind wasn't cooperating. Soon, this entire side of Vaughn would be nothing but ashes.

"I'm not an agent anymore, and Zeus is a purebred bull terrier. I'm the only one who gets to call him a mutt." Granger's heart pumped harder every minute they didn't have eyes on Charlie or his K9 partner. "And that mutt is a better hunter than you'll ever be, Acker. Dress it up any way you like, you need me and my partner to help find Charlie."

Henry Acker had no problem keeping up. Despite the grief from losing one daughter in the past week and the effects of age, the man had stayed physically fit. At least enough to keep up a panicked search for Charlie.

"If we don't, the last thing you'll be worrying about is your dog."

Granger didn't have time for petty offenses. Charlie was out here. She had to be. Acker's men hadn't reported any conflicts with intruders other than Granger and Charlie in the past twenty-four hours, which meant those gunshots had been meant for her. And the thought of her out here—alone, possibly injured—pushed him harder. Socorro wasn't going to get here in time. He had to rely on Acker's Army to recover Charlie. "The *Sangre por Sangre* cartel has surveillance photos of Charlie. They've been following her ever since she came back to New Mexico three days ago."

Henry Acker didn't respond.

"But you already knew that, didn't you?" Granger pulled up short. As much as he hated to stop the search for Charlie, he had to know what they were walking into. He turned on Charlie's father as his anger built. The son of a bitch put his family at risk, and for what? To make a statement? For power? "You got into bed with a drug cartel. They came here tonight to get to her. All this time, you knew exactly what they were capable of, and you refused to protect your own daughters from falling into their hands."

Acker suddenly seemed so much smaller than Granger remembered. Unsure of himself. It was a mere glimpse of the man behind the army, but in an instant, that glimpse was gone. Henry Acker rolled his shoulders back, once again every inch the man Charlie had described. "The last thing I'm going to do is explain myself to the federal agent who used one of my daughters to get to me and the people I protect."

The accusation stabbed deep. Because Henry Acker was right. Granger had used Charlie just as her father had used her: to fight a war nobody could win. "What does the cartel want from her? What are they planning? What do they need her for?"

"It doesn't matter. They won't kill her. At least not until they get what they want." Acker maneuvered around Granger and picked up the pace. "Charlie is strong. She'll hold her own against interrogation just the way I taught her."

Granger had been put through interrogation training during his stint with Homeland Security, and he didn't want to think about Charlie strapped to a chair and physically tortured until she broke. And now she was potentially in the hands of *Sangre por Sangre*, the most bloodthirsty and brutal drug cartel Granger and Socorro had faced. There was nothing in the world he wouldn't give up to ensure Charlie never had to go through that kind of nightmare. "Everyone has a breaking point."

"If you truly believe that, then you don't know my daughter." Henry Acker kept moving, the topic reaching its end.

Movement registered up ahead. Granger reached for Acker's elbow, but the man was already slowing down to get a better read. A whine filtered in through the rustle of trees.

"Zeus?" The K9's yip spiked Granger's pulse. He maneuvered around Henry Acker and stepped into a clearing. Searching for signs of an ambush, he grabbed onto

Zeus's collar. The bull terrier barked, unfazed by the appearance of his handler. "What do you have, bud?"

Another bark—louder this time—triggered a ringing in Granger's ears. Granger ran his hands over the dog's frame to check for wounds and turned Zeus's head toward him. A ring of something wet and dark disrupted the pattern along the dog's face. Granger swiped it from the K9's fur, rubbing it between both fingers. "He's got something." Granger shoved to stand, facing off with Acker. "Blood. Whoever Zeus attacked, he caused some damage."

"I'm starting to like that dog." Acker pushed ahead. "He's trying to tell you they went this way, but something is keeping him from following. Like he's been told to stay."

"Zeus doesn't listen to anyone but me." His confidence waned as he took in the K9's restlessness. Zeus had been trained to follow Granger's commands from the time he was a pup. Then again, Granger had never given anyone else the chance to try. It'd taken months for the bull terrier to establish trust in Granger. There's no way Charlie could've done it in mere hours. Right?

"A lot of people underestimate my daughter's influence." Acker shouldered his rifle and forged ahead. "Take it from me. I made that mistake once. Cost me something I loved in the end."

Granger found himself trying to keep up with the Acker patriarch. He whistled for his partner, and the K9 followed on his heels. "Go get her, Zeus."

The dog launched off his back legs and shot into the trees.

"These woods spill out onto barren desert in less than a quarter mile." Henry Acker called back over his shoulder. "My guess, they're trying to get her out of Vaughn from there by ATV or vehicle. The fire was a distraction."

And a damn good one at that. If what Granger believed about Henry Acker was true and the bastard had gotten into bed with a drug cartel, *Sangre por Sangre* had to know the kind of manpower and firepower Acker's Army carried. Threatening the town they'd die to protect was the only way to take the focus off the cartel's real intentions: getting to Charlie.

"Your daughter Erin." They moved by the light of the fire at their backs. Both in line as they followed after Zeus. "When the cartel couldn't find Charlie, they came for her, didn't they? They knew she'd been involved in the pipeline explosion, that she had her own expertise from the attack."

Henry Acker pushed the pace, refusing to confirm Granger's theory. "We're almost there. Be ready."

Battle-ready tension filtered down Granger's spine.

The trees were thinning up ahead. They broke through the border.

A pair of headlights skimmed across the desert.

Acker and the two soldiers behind them opened fire on the vehicle. Metallic pings sparked off the side of the armored SUV.

Return fire pulverized the dirt at their feet.

Granger grabbed for the old man and hauled him out of the way of the oncoming bullets. He threw Acker behind one of the last trees for cover.

"What the hell are you doing? My daughter is in

there." Acker raised his rifle and got off another two rounds, but his rifle wouldn't be strong enough to breach through that armor.

Two more sets of headlights flared to life. Engines rumbled across the desert floor and exposed a game of hide-and-seek. Damn it. Charlie could be in any of one the SUVs. "I'm saving your life, Acker. *Sangre por Sangre* only moves in packs, and they don't travel light. Those vehicles are armored. You'll never get through."

"So you're just going to let them get away." Henry Acker took another shot from behind the tree.

"Hell, no." Granger pulled his cell phone from his pocket as all three SUV's shot into the dark unknown of the desert. A single bar of service lit up the screen. It was enough. He dialed in to Socorro. The line connected. "Scarlett, I need my SUV."

"Narrowing down your location." Static punctured through each of Socorro's security expert's words. "Got you. Sending it your way. ETA two minutes. Just enough time for you to tell me what the hell is going on. I can see the fire from here."

"No time to explain." Two minutes. Socorro was in route. They'd responded to Zeus's alert. Damn it. *Sangre por Sangre* was already moving at full speed. They didn't have that kind of time. "Redirect your approach on my position to intercept three hostile vehicles with a hostage inside."

"You got it." Scarlett ended the call just as a fourth pair of headlights cut into Granger's peripheral vision.

"Come on, old man." He pulled Acker out from the cover of the trees. The SUV pulled to a stop ten feet ahead of them, and Granger wrenched the driver's side door open. "Get in."

Henry Acker collapsed into the passenger seat, his weapon folded across his lap, jaw slack. "Had I known this thing could drive itself, I would've had the boys strip it for parts."

Granger threw the SUV into gear, chasing after three pairs of distinct brake lights a mile ahead. Momentum pinned him to his seat as they sped across the desert floor. "It's only accessible through Socorro's security system. Besides, I think you got enough of a donation from me out of the cargo area."

"And Acker's Army thanks you kindly." Acker turned in his seat as two more sets of headlights filtered in through the back window. "Those your people?"

"They're not shooting at us, so I think it's safe to believe they're here to help." He checked the rearview mirror, hit the radio tied into his steering wheel and floored the accelerator. He wasn't going to screw this up. Not like he had the night of the Alamo pipeline attack. Charlie was coming home safe. "Scarlett, you take the right. I've got the center. Tell whoever's with you to take the left."

"You got it." The SUVs on his tail maneuvered into position and raced ahead. Within seconds, each vehicle had cut off the *Sangre por Sangre* caravan and brought them to a halt.

"Stay in the vehicle." Granger pulled a weapon from underneath the seat, happy to know Acker's Army wasn't all that adept at searching for weapons.

"Like hell I am." Acker shouldered out of the SUV

and hit the ground, rifle raised as both Scarlett and another Socorro operative took the *Sangre por Sangre* drivers out of their vehicles.

"Clear," Scarlett said. Two Dobermans circled the driver on the ground with his hands on the back of his head.

"Clear." Recognition flared as Granger identified Socorro's forward scout, Cash Meyers, and his K9, Bear. "I've got nothing."

Granger approached the third vehicle. He reached for the vehicle's handle and nearly ripped the door off its hinges. Pulling the driver from behind the steering wheel, he planted the cartel soldier on the ground. "Where is she?"

Scarlett rushed to search the back of the third vehicle, lowering her weapon. "Granger... She's not here."

Chapter Eight

Her brain struggled to stay awake. She was so tired.

The vibration of an engine shook through her as Charlie stared up at the ceiling of the SUV. She'd tried replaying the moment everything had gone wrong, but it was just a waste of energy. Her attacker had won. In the end, she hadn't been strong enough.

Now Granger and Zeus were at risk.

Her father's life was in danger.

And she would be forced to do something terrible for the cartel.

Her frame bounced along the back seat of the vehicle, absorbing the uneven terrain. Every shift aggravated the pain in her body. The bruises were already pulsing. Her face most likely looked like a jar of spaghetti sauce. She could taste the blood at the back of her throat. And she had...nothing left.

Charlie twisted against the rope secured around her wrists. Seemed drug cartels knew better than to use zip ties. Too easily broken. The rope would take time for her to get through. Especially when she couldn't keep her eyes open.

After everything she'd fought to leave behind, the

past refused to stay where it belonged. What had been the point of running? Memories she promised never to recall surged forward with the slightest effort. She didn't have the strength to stop them now.

That night had changed her life. And taken the lives of four others. She knew their names, had memorized their faces. She'd attended the funerals, out of sight, despite the risk of Homeland Security or her family learning she hadn't been caught in the explosion. She'd learned about the families they'd left behind and worked two separate jobs to send them money every month. It'd been the least she could do to help replace the income they'd lost after the attack. Though it could never be enough.

She'd seen Granger at every single one of the services to pay his respects, and his stoic grief had felt contagious and deep and uncomfortable. At times, she'd imagined that grief had been for her, and it'd taken years to convince herself that Sage was right. That she'd been foolish to believe he wanted her for anything more than a resource. His confidential informant. The nights they'd spent together—the secret rendezvous—had most likely been surveilled and authorized by Homeland Security, and she'd gone right along with it for the chance of having something for herself. Something nobody in her family knew about, something that made her more than a soldier.

I was in love with you too.

Had he really said that? It was hard to remember as the pain in her face and head peaked. The burning sensation in her calf told her the bleeding from the bullet had stopped but that she wouldn't get far if she managed to escape. Swirls of shapes danced behind her eyes. The kind that warned her she was about to fall asleep.

But she couldn't.

Because she believed him when Granger had said he'd loved her. That he'd been searching for her. That he knew without a doubt she hadn't died in that explosion. He was out there, looking for her right now. Risking his and Zeus's lives for her in the middle of a forest fire. Not only against the people who took her but the terrorist army determined to bring down anyone associated with the US government. And she was just going to give up?

No. Granger deserved better than the woman who'd run at the slightest obstacle in their path all those years ago. She wasn't that person anymore. And she wasn't afraid.

"I'm going to be sick." Charlie fought against the momentum of the vehicle and coughed up the acid lodged in her throat onto the floor.

"Hey! I'm going to have to clean that up." Her abductor turned in his seat as she lost the contents in her stomach. The SUV's course deviated, and he jerked the wheel back in place.

She pulled at the rope around her hands to test the slack. Grainy fibers scratched at the thin skin there, but she managed to create space. Enough to slide one of the seat belt buckles between her wrists. If she pulled with enough force, there was a chance the metal could cut through the rope. "Stop the car. Please. I don't feel well."

Charlie started coughing again, ducking her head between the edge of the back seat and the rear of the front. Her abductor hit the brakes, and she had to plant her shoulder to keep from sliding to the floor. Only the SUV hadn't pulled to a complete stop.

Her abductor's swollen gaze moved to the rearview mirror. Blood crusted around his nose and face, and a small thread of victory charged through her. For as much damage as he'd done to her, she was pleased to see she'd gotten a couple shots in. The SUV lurched forward and exceeded its previous speed, as though he'd spotted something closing in. Or someone. "I recommend you swallow whatever comes up. We're not stopping."

For the first time, Charlie realized the interior of the SUV was darker than usual. No light coming from the instrument panel. Nothing ahead. They were driving without headlights. To make an escape. "Granger."

He was alive. He was coming for her.

The drugging effects of trauma dissipated slower than she wanted, but they were receding, second by second. Granger wouldn't be able to see the SUV as long as the headlights remained off.

If she wanted out of this in one piece, she'd have to earn his attention.

Charlie angled herself a few inches off the back seat. Her ribs screamed for relief, but she couldn't think about that right now. The rope caught against the empty seat buckle, and she pulled at it with everything she had left. Which wasn't much, but the threads were already coming apart. Holding her breath, she kept her gaze on the driver and tried again. Another bit of rope unraveled. At this rate, she'd secure the use of her hands after her abductor delivered her to the cartel.

She gritted through the pain flaring through her upper

body. She could do this. She *had* to do this. For the sake of all those people who would pay the price if *Sangre por Sangre* won. Lightning struck behind her eyes as the last of the rope broke free. Feeling surged into her hands, and she took her first full breath since being hauled into the vehicle.

The driver wasn't going to stop. He wasn't going to slow down, but throwing herself from the vehicle was sure to finish the job he'd started back in those woods. She couldn't wait until they arrived wherever the hell they were going either, and the longer she thought it over, the less chance she'd have of escape.

This had to happen now.

Where Granger still might be able to get to her.

Charlie slowly brought her hands in front of her so as not to attract the driver's attention, keeping under his visual radar. Her breath shook through her as she considered the consequences of her next move. It was going to hurt. If she survived. Untwining the sections of rope from around her wrists, she reworked the longest piece between both hands.

And launched forward.

She hooked the rope around the driver's seat and over her abductor's head. He grabbed for the stranglehold she had on him, but Charlie used his own seat to protect herself. The fibers dug deep into his skin as gasps escaped. A part of his brain knew to keep one hand on the steering wheel while attempting to lighten the weight on his throat with the other. But his automatic need to leverage his weight into the seat floored the accelerator. They were speeding up. In complete darkness.

The rope cut into her hands. Just a few more seconds. She didn't want to kill him. She just needed him unconscious. Her abductor let his hand drop away from the steering wheel. The vehicle slowed without his constant pressure on the accelerator. He was losing consciousness.

Relief loosened the hold she had on the rope. It was going to work.

Her abductor pulled a blade. He sliced through the rope at his neck. His loud gasp punctured through the interior of the car.

Charlie fell back in the seat with nothing but two pieces of severed rope in her hand. The vehicle charged forward, pinning her to the seat, but she couldn't give up. She had to get out of here. She dove for the front seat.

The blade came up to meet her.

Hot steel sliced through her sweat-drenched shirt and across skin. Charlie fell into the passenger side door. She kicked at her abductor's wrist. The blade slammed against the opposite window with a crack. The window shattered, spewing tiny shards of glass into their seats. She kicked at him again. "Stop the car!"

But he wasn't listening. The driver blocked her next strike.

She went for the keys and knocked the steering wheel.

Shapes took form ahead through the windshield.

Rock formations.

They were driving straight into the side of a mountain.

"Look out!" Charlie grabbed for her seat belt and locked it in.

The driver's face lit up with panic.

Just before impact.

The SUV slammed into rock. The whole world turned upside down as the back of the vehicle vaulted upward. Charlie braced herself against the dashboard. Seconds seemed to turn into minutes as glass cut through the inside of the car.

The impact jolted through every cell in her body as the ceiling caved in. Metal screeched and ripped apart under the cutting edge of the rocks. The vehicle rolled. Once. Twice. The windshield cracked but held its own. Pain and nausea took control as the SUV jumped the formation and jerked downward into some kind of ravine. Gravity seemed to have lost its hold with each flip.

Until they weren't moving at all.

The SUV groaned as it settled. Charlie reached one hand out, looking for something to hold onto, but nothing seemed to be where it was supposed to be. The seat belt cut into her hips and shoulder, locking her in place upside down. She was conscious enough to realize she was still alive. That she'd survived, but the pain… Her body was trying to shut down to manage the trauma. Sooner or later, she wouldn't be able to fight it.

The smell of gas permeated her senses.

The fuel lines… They must have ruptured. She had to get out before any of the hot engine parts sparked a fire. Pressure built in her head as she reached for the seat belt latch. It released. She dropped shoulder-first onto the warped and torn metal ceiling with a cry. Tears burned in her eyes as she fixated on the passenger side window. It'd lost its shape in the crash. It wasn't big enough to crawl through. She'd have to find another way.

Charlie caught sight of the driver. Dead or unconscious, she didn't know, and she didn't want to find out. She forced her body between both front seats and clawed into the back. The cargo area had been saved. She could get out through there.

Every movement aggravated a deep pain she'd never experienced. Blinding and strong. But soon she'd made it to the cargo area. She tried the latch, but it wouldn't release.

Smoke filtered through the vents from the front of the vehicle.

She turned. Just as the SUV's engine caught fire.

GRANGER FLIPPED THE driver of the third SUV onto his back and took aim. "Where is she? Where is Charlie Acker?"

The soldier relaxed against the desert floor, laughing. "You'll never find her, *mercenario. Sangre por Sangre* owns her now."

"Like hell they do." Henry Acker fisted the driver's shirt and hauled the soldier up, slamming him against the car. "I'm going to give you three seconds to tell us where my daughter is, amigo, or you won't live to see the sunrise. Got it?"

"I'm willing to die for my cause," the cartel soldier said. "If you'd kept your end of our deal, you daughter wouldn't have to die for yours."

"What deal?" Granger closed the distance between them, both Socorro operatives and their K9s doing the same. The pieces were starting to fit together. Slower than he wanted, but sure all the same. "What the hell is he talking about, Acker?"

"Nothing." Contained anger slipped into Acker's eyes. "There is no deal. He's lying to stall us from getting to Charlie. That's his job. To slow us down."

"I don't have time for this. Scarlett, watch them." Granger shoved Acker away from the cartel soldier and confiscated the old man's weapon. He whistled for Zeus, and the dog targeted Henry Acker. The bull terrier latched onto the man's pants and dragged the patriarch to the ground. Zeus ripped and pulled back and forth.

"Get your damn dog off me!" Acker tried escaping the K9's hold, but it was no use. He kicked at the ground with both feet. Nothing but Granger's command would set the dog to release.

Scarlett and her Dobermans stood guard on the three drivers meant to distract them.

Granger stood over Acker as fear laced every aged line in the man's face. Zeus could kill him if Granger deemed it appropriate, but right now, all he wanted was the truth. "Tell me about the deal you made with the cartel."

"There is no deal!" Acker struggled for freedom, but Granger wasn't finished with him yet. "I'll kill you for this, Morais. Every single one of you."

"And our little dogs too. I've heard it all before," he said. "Zeus, want to play your favorite game?"

The bull terrier's mouth curled into an excited smile as his tail started whipping back and forth. Zeus followed direct orders, launching his entire weight across Acker's torso. The old man's resulting groan for breath was enough to trigger an automatic inhale in Granger.

"Let's try that again, Acker." Granger crouched beside Charlie's father. "What deal did Acker's Army make with *Sangre por Sangre*?"

"Support. I agreed to supply them with manpower and weapons," Acker said.

"To do what?" The answer was already there, waiting for him to come to the realization himself. "You were going to attack the state capital building, weren't you? That's what was on those blueprints Charlie stole. All the notes you'd made. You and the cartel were going to raid the biggest government building in the state in an attempt to reestablish *Sangre por Sangre*'s cartel. That's what this is about. It's a power grab."

"No." Acker fought to breathe, but Zeus's massive weight wasn't going anywhere. "It's not the capital building they're interested in. That was just the first step."

"You put your daughter's life at risk for your own greed, Acker." The accusation burned hotter than the fire they'd just escaped. He pointed a hard finger into the man's chest. "Whatever happens to her, that's on you, and I hope you live with that guilt for the rest of your life."

"Granger." Scarlett penetrated his peripheral vision.

"Not now." They were so close to answers. He and the rest of Socorro had run *Sangre por Sangre* into the ground. This was the final piece they needed to eradicate the cartel's influence for good.

"Granger, look." Scarlett's insistence was enough to break his focus on Acker.

He shoved to his feet. And caught sight of a fire in the distance. Instinct kicked him into action. What were the chances of two fires set in the middle of nowhere?

His gut said whatever was going on had something to do with Charlie. That she was out there. That she was still alive. "Zeus, car."

The bull terrier released his prisoner and raced for the car. The K9's back feet slipped on the frame of the SUV, but he managed to get himself inside. Granger hauled Henry Acker to his feet and practically shoved him into the back of Scarlett's SUV. "You're staying here. I might've used Charlie in order to do my job all those years ago, same as you, but there's a difference between us. I'm the one who's trying to protect her now."

A flood of grief and shame replaced the anger that'd flared in the patriarch's expression, but Granger wasn't the person to offer anything comforting. This entire night had led to one goal: bringing Charlie home safe. "I'm going out there."

"You have no idea what you're going up against," Cash said.

"I'll be fine. There aren't enough of us to detain these drivers and keep Acker from doing something stupid." He dropped the magazine from his weapon with the touch of a button and counted the rounds left inside. Slamming the mag back into place, he holstered the sidearm on his hip. "Get what you can out of Acker. Tie him up if you have to. Stopping *Sangre por Sangre* from whatever they're planning is all that matters."

"Be careful out there." Scarlett stepped back, hugging her rifle to her vest. "We've got things covered. Just go do what you have to do."

Granger nodded goodbye and climbed into the driver's seat of his SUV. In seconds, he and Zeus were charging toward the glow of the fire. Because that worked out so well the first time.

The K9 whined from the front seat as Granger hyper focused on the fire less than a mile out.

He scrubbed his hand between Zeus's ears, but there was nothing he could do or say to neutralize the acidic worry in his stomach. "I know. We're going to find her. I promise. We're all she has left."

The thought of Charlie suffering alone had him bringing the SUV to its top speed. There was nothing but scrub brush, Joshua trees and dirt out here, but something had happened. Smoke filtered through his SUV's vents the closer he came to the fire. Only there was no visual sign of a source.

He carved the headlights along the rock formations guarding a drop on the other side. Chunks of metal and glass reflected back. Holy hell. Granger slammed his foot against the brake, nearly tipping Zeus into the front console. He shoved the vehicle into Park as dread pooled at the base of his spine. "No, no, no, no, no."

Granger shouldered free of the SUV, not bothering to close the driver's side door behind him, and ran for the wreckage. Glass crunched beneath his boots. The scent of gasoline filled his lungs. A single vehicle had rammed into the rock formation and tipped into the dried-up ravine. And now that car was on fire. "Charlie!"

She didn't answer.

Granger couldn't wait for his training to warn him about going into a deadly situation without knowing all the details. If she was down there, she had mere seconds to get out before the whole thing blew.

Flames crawled around the engine block and shot up into the sky. Fortunately, there was nothing out here to catch fire. Not like the woods around her childhood home. But an accelerated fire would explode if it reached the gas tank. Gravity pulled him down the incline to the bottom of the ravine.

Smoke had filled the interior and blocked out the windows. She was here. She had to be. Zeus's bark from the top of the hill echoed along the floor of the riverbed. The driver's side window had been pulverized, but there was no sign of a driver.

Granger checked each of the other windows, but it was too hard to see inside. The doors were stuck, too damaged from the accident. Unholstering his sidearm, he protected his face from the flames lashing out from the front of the vehicle. "Hold on, Charlie. Just hold on."

Granger slammed the butt of his weapon into the back driver's side window. The first strike merely cracked the glass. He tried again. The second shattered the protective layer, and a rush of smoke billowed into his face. "Charlie, are you in there?"

Black smoke cleared enough to give him a view of a single hand resting between the cargo area and the back seats of the SUV. Unmoving. Granger was already trying to rip the door off its hinges. The car refused to budge. "I'm coming for you. Hang on!"

He rounded to the back of the vehicle and brought the butt of his weapon up. There was a chance the glass windshield would slice through her clothing on impact, but Granger didn't have any other choice. He rammed the metal against the glass. Then again. And again. The glass was stronger here. Pain cut through his rib cage from the bullet graze, taking some of his strength. He was running out of time.

Zeus's incessant barking wouldn't let up. Every concerned sound notched Granger's nerves a level higher until he couldn't focus on anything but getting to Charlie.

He threw everything he had into the next strike.

The glass finally gave up the ghost.

Granger used the barrel of his weapon to knock the rest of the glass around the edge of the frame free and reached inside for the hatch. And pulled. The cargo door hydraulics kicked into gear, and he dove inside.

Dragging Charlie's lean body by both ankles, he hauled her over his shoulder and ran for the incline up to the rock formations. The bullet graze in his side threatened to rip wider, and a growl of pain escaped his throat. The fire was spreading along the SUV's frame. He had to move.

A hiss reached his ears.

A split second before the vehicle exploded.

Glass, metal and fire split in a thousand different directions. The pressure fanned out, and Granger was forced to dive for the side of the incline. He'd only made it half way to Zeus's position above. Right in the explosion's path. Curling around Charlie, he used his body as protection against incoming debris and fisted his hands into the dirt on either side of her head.

Heat fanned up the back of his legs and spine, but he wouldn't let any of it touch her. Ever. The fire seemed to suction back in on itself after another minute, and cool air filtered across his skin.

"Granger?" Her voice sounded so weak compared to the woman he'd found barricaded in her safe house.

Granger held the weight of his upper body away from her, staring down at the bloody damage she'd sustained fighting for her life. "It's okay. I've got you. You're safe."

She brought her hands up as the fire reflected off the glimmer of tears in her eyes. "The driver. He took me. He wants to use me to help the cartel. He wants me to do something awful. Tell me you have him."

Driver? Granger had checked the vehicle. "Charlie, there was no driver."

Chapter Nine

Her abductor had gotten away.

Charlie flinched away from the light shining in her eyes.

"Any headaches, nausea, vomiting, memory problems?" The physician cut the light to her other eye, looking for what, Charlie didn't know. Piel. That was her name. Dr. Piel. Socorro's on-call doctor. Though Charlie couldn't exactly remember coming to this place. The woman's gloved touch was gentle but probing around her broken nose and split lip.

"Would you judge me if I said yes to all of the above?" The pounding pain at the back of her eyes receded with the light, and Charlie was able to take in the room she'd woken up in. Crisp, clean walls and cabinets but comfortable-looking seating. The hospital bed itself didn't feel like the one she'd found herself in from time to time when her father's training had gone too far. Then again, the people of Vaughn relied on a single physician who lived within town and had committed himself to the cause. His idea of a recovery room was his teenage son's bedroom. A kid Charlie had beaten the crap out of more times than she could count while sparring.

Not to mention that place didn't have anything close to a heart monitor or dimmable lighting. It was meant to be a way station. A temporary stop to make sure she hadn't sustained permanent damage. This place felt... good. Safe. Though she didn't know enough about Socorro or the people who worked here to come to that conclusion, she couldn't deny the sense of security she felt inside these walls.

"Not at all." The physician took a seat on a rolling stool. Long thin fingers made notes on a tablet resting in Dr. Piel's lap. Smooth black hair framed pristinely shaped eyebrows and almond-shaped eyes. The doctor was thin though Charlie couldn't ignore the way her arms filled out the sleeves of her white coat. A physician who worked for the top private military contractor in the country most likely knew how to hold her own in a fight. "I can definitively tell that you've sustained a concussion. Most likely from all the times you ran your face into someone's fist."

"Just couldn't seem to help myself." Though now Charlie was feeling the full effect of those punches. Effects from the car accident too. She tried to shift her weight to sit up straighter, but her hands, hips and legs weren't too interested in movement.

Dr. Piel smiled. "Don't worry. It isn't as severe as it feels. Concussions are something I see a lot of around here. If I was smart, I'd go back to school and shift my specialty to neurology for how many times operatives come in here with head injuries. You just need some rest. The smoke inhalation you suffered caused some lung irritation, but that should clear up in the next twenty-four hours, and as for the bullet graze on your leg, you'll survive. For now, I need you to stay awake. I'll be able to reset your nose when the swelling goes down in a couple hours."

That was when the fun would really start.

"I imagine it's nonstop around here, considering their line of work." Charlie focused on the softness of the sheets rather than the fact her clothes had been taken from her.

"Pretty much." Dr. Piel rolled to a built-in desk on the other side of the room. "You'd think they'd learn their lesson, but they just keep coming back. Concussions, stab wounds, gunshot wounds. I've seen it all."

"What about Granger?" She shouldn't have asked, but the words had already slipped out, the haze of exhaustion throwing her common sense out the door. "Have you seen him for any of those?"

"That would be covered under doctor-patient confidentiality." Dr. Piel stood, her expression losing its humor from a minute ago. "But what I *can* tell you is that Granger and the rest have sustained a lot of wounds doing what they do. It's admirable really. How hard they fight for the people they care about and some they don't even know. I'm proud to be the one who helps them keep going."

Silence seeped between them as Charlie considered her words.

"Try to get some rest." The good doctor settled a hand on Charlie's shoulder in an attempt to offer some kind of comfort, but how was she supposed to come to terms with what she'd gone through just a few hours ago? "I'll bring you something for the pain and try to convince Granger he can wait a little longer before seeing you."

"He's out there?" A sliver of need charged through her.

"Has been this entire time." Dr. Piel turned her tablet toward Charlie to show her the screen. The doctor scrolled through what seemed like a thousand small blue message bubbles. "Keeps messaging me, asking how you're doing. Do you want to see him?"

"Yes. Please." Her emotions were starting to show. She couldn't hide how much she needed Granger in the same room as her. To convince herself this was real. That she'd survived. That this wasn't some dream.

"I'll send him in." Dr. Piel gave her a knowing smile. Quick but warm. She headed for the door, pulling it open. "But I still want you to get some rest. No activities that take a lot of brain power. That means no TV, reading or general merriment in any shape or form. I'll be right back with that pain medication."

"Thank you." And before she was able to sit herself up in expectation of company, he was there.

Every bruise and laceration stood out under the overhead lighting. He looked battle-worn and on the verge of collapse, but Granger had waited outside her room until given the all clear to come in. He'd gone to war for her—up against her father's men and an entire cartel bent on using her for their own gain—and if he hadn't pulled her out of that SUV, she would've died. "Hi."

It was all she could manage in the moment, overtaken by the sheer sight of him. It'd been like that the moment they'd met. Having him here when she felt at her lowest was drugging and addictive and a relief.

"Hi." His voice weighed heavy with exhaustion, but Granger managed to close the distance between them. He angled himself onto the edge of the bed. "What's the diagnosis? Anything serious?"

"I'll live." Because going into detail was bound to send her into a tailspin if she wasn't careful, and Charlie didn't want to ruin this moment. She just wanted him. To feel something other than pain, to enjoy the fact they made it through one more day. Together. She brought her hand to his temple, where one of the soldiers from Acker's Army had clocked him. "How are you?"

"I'll live." His laugh rumbled down her hand and into her chest. Granger slid his calloused palm over her fingers, leaning into her touch. "Damn, you feel good."

"But I probably smell horrible." The scent of smoke and dirt and gasoline combined into a noxious odor on her skin and in her hair. He had to have sustained brain damage not to pick up on it.

"I don't mind." He turned his mouth into her hand and planted a kiss at her wrist. Right where the rope she'd been tied with had scratched her skin. "Nothing about you is as bad as Zeus's gas after one of his binge-eating episodes."

Her laugh caught her by surprise and aggravated the bone-deep pain running throughout her body. A piece of her wanted this moment to freeze. She wanted to pretend *Sangre por Sangre* hadn't almost killed her, threatened her father and might've had something to do with her sister's death. If it were up to her, she would ignore the pressure in her chest and stretch these precious life-affirming minutes out as long as she could. Because she deserved it. After a decade of isolating herself and looking over her shoulder, she just wanted a few minutes to remind herself she was human. But that wasn't how she was built. "Did your team find anything at the site of the crash?"

Granger lost the softness at the edges of his eyes. Threading his hand in hers, he dragged her hand into his lap. "Our logistics operative got Fire and Rescue out there to take care of the fire before it spread. Two other members of my team searched the area, but there was no sign of remains once the fire was out. Hard to tell with the rocky terrain, but it looks like whoever abducted you escaped."

"And they'll try again." She couldn't bury the shudder running from the top of her spine to her toes.

"Hey. You're safe here." Gravel seemed to coat every word out of his mouth. "I give you my word the cartel will never lay another hand on you."

"Except this isn't your fight, Granger." No matter how much she needed it to be. No matter how much she needed him at her side. "I came back to figure out who killed my sister. My father has plans to attack the state capitol, and a drug cartel wants to use me to put them back in power. None of this has anything to do with you. I'm the one who has to bring it to an end."

"Who the hell said you have to do it alone?" he asked.

She didn't have an answer for that. In truth, she'd simply taken it all upon herself. "You almost died out there in those woods. I just… I don't want to have to go through the process of losing you all over again."

It'd hurt too much the first time. She wasn't sure she

could make it through again. If she could tolerate the isolation, the lies she would have to tell, the pain.

"I'm not going anywhere, Charlie." He stared down at their hands, intertwined. Ash and dirt and blood stained the fabric of his pants, and right then, Charlie understood it to be a perfect representation of their history. "You ran away from me once because you were afraid our relationship meant nothing to me. I'm not the kind of man who makes the same mistake twice."

He brought her hand to his mouth and kissed the thin scratched skin along the back. Warmth speared down her arm and tightened her insides. His next kiss was at her forearm. He moved closer, following the length of her arm with his mouth. The coarse hair along his jaw tickled her neck as he buried his face between her shoulder and jaw. And still he didn't stop.

Until he reached her mouth.

SHE TASTED JUST as he remembered. No. Even better.

It almost felt wrong to take advantage of her physical state right now, but the time without her—the past ten years, and the devastating hour during which she'd been taken—was about to destroy him. The only solution was this. This moment. This connection they'd lost themselves in once before. It'd been the only thing that'd grounded him the night of the Alamo pipeline explosion. That'd kept him from losing his mind, and he had the chance to feel that again. With her.

He couldn't fix what'd gone wrong in their lives. He wanted to. With every cell in his body, he wanted to make it so she wasn't in pain, so she didn't have this invisible target on her back. Maybe if he'd followed his gut and reached out the night of the attack, despite their agreement to keep their distance, he could've prevented all of this from happening. He could've protected her, and she wouldn't have gone through what she had tonight. She wouldn't have had to be alone these past ten years.

Instead, they were sharing a desperate kiss he couldn't seem to break. And she was kissing him back, pulling him deeper into an endless well of need he wasn't sure they'd ever be able to escape. Damn it, if he were being honest with himself, he didn't want to. Because this, right here, was his version of heaven. Free of fear, free of the weight of loss and loneliness. They deserved this. A small freedom from the terror that waited outside these walls, and suddenly, she was all there was, and Granger never wanted this moment to end, like so many others had.

They'd survived. Together. He'd lived despite every obstacle in their way. For this moment. For this woman. In this room, he no longer felt invincible as he had in the field, but very, very human. Alive. As though he'd just regained feeling that had been lost since the night she'd disappeared. Like he'd been waiting to breathe all this time.

Charlie speared battered hands through his hair, holding him in place, mirroring his need to hold her as close as possible. Her exhale shook through her, uncontrolled, caged. She broke the kiss and set her forehead against his. "I've missed you so much."

"I missed you too." Whatever happened after this didn't matter. Because this moment was perfect. It was theirs, and nothing in the world could take that from them. They weren't their pasts. The future didn't exist yet. He just needed to be here. "You have no idea how much."

Charlie bit down on her bottom lip then flinched against the pain of the split. "If you feel anything like I do right now, I think I might have some idea."

A throat cleared from near the door. "Perhaps you should wait before you start undressing each other." Ivy Bardot stood tall, chin parallel to the floor, as she waited for them to separate.

His chest felt as though it would break apart if he released his hold on Charlie. Granger peeled his hand from her arm, instantly aware of the empty sensation forging through him. He added a bit of distance between them but didn't bother removing himself from the bed. "You need me?"

"I wouldn't be interrupting your reunion if this weren't important." Socorro's founder didn't wait for an answer as she turned on her impossibly high heels and wrenched the door open before stepping into the hallway.

"I'll be right back." He needed Charlie to know that. That he wasn't going anywhere. That he would fight for her all over again. Granger pressed a kiss to her forehead. Though not for her reassurance. For his. Then he followed Ivy out. "I requested twenty-four hours off the clock. Last time I checked, I'm not on duty."

"Henry Acker isn't talking," Ivy said.

"He taught everyone in his backward army to hold up against interrogation. Charlie included." He nodded through the window looking into Charlie's recovery room. "From what I understand, he's damn good at it too. Stands to reason he'd use the same techniques in case of capture."

"Let me rephrase that." Ivy turned to face him, seemingly watching for every change in his expression, every unintentional tick. "Henry Acker won't talk to anyone but his daughter."

His gut hollowed as the events of the past twelve hours carved through his brain. "Charlie has been through hell because of that man. There's no way I'm going to make her face him after what she's gone through. He can sit in the interrogation room as long as it takes to get to him to open up. I'm not putting her recovery at risk."

"Is that really up to you?" Ivy cut her attention to the window, watching the woman on the other side. "You care about her, that much is clear. But Henry Acker knows details about *Sangre por Sangre*'s plans. There's a chance he's the only one who knows, and we need that information if we're going to carry out our mission here."

"You want me to use her to get to him." A sick feeling knotted in his gut as the past threatened to overtake the present. Charlie had just come back into his life. He couldn't risk losing her again. "I did that once, Ivy. I turned her into a CI who started working against the very people who'd raised her, and I lost her for ten years. How can you ask me to do that to her again?"

"I'm not asking *you*." Ivy kept her voice even. No emotion. Nothing but logic. "I'm asking her to the make the choice. The same choice you gave her all those years ago."

"I shouldn't have recruited her in the first place. If I

hadn't, maybe none of this would be happening now," he said.

"Or maybe it would, and we wouldn't have a way to stop this attack. This game we're playing can't be won with what-ifs." Ivy crossed her arms. "I know what you're thinking, Granger. I know how important she is to you, but you have to remember what's at stake here. We have nothing but a set of charred blueprints of the state capitol with notes we can't decipher. Without Henry Acker's statement concerning the cartel's motives, we are operating blind. Everything we've done these past two years—everyone's lives that were lost in this fight to bring down the cartel—will be for nothing if we let *Sangre por Sangre* regain even an inch of ground. We've come so close, and I can't let us lose now. There's too much at risk. You have your orders."

Ivy's footsteps echoed off the black tile mazing through every square foot of this place.

"You mean our source inside the cartel is at risk." Granger didn't bother facing her. The click of her heels had stopped. He had never stood up to Socorro's founder before, but there was a piece of him that knew he could've protected Charlie better had he had the guts to stand up to his supervisory agent at Homeland. No one above him would sign off on labeling her as his CI. Too much of a risk. No matter how many times he'd tried to push the paperwork through, they denied him. So he'd done what he'd had to to convince her she was protected, that the government would have her back in case anything went sideways. He'd taken the risk on personally, knowing it wouldn't be enough. And in the end, he'd failed her. "That's what this is about for you, isn't it? Getting him out alive?"

Ivy didn't have an answer for that.

Granger turned, leaning against the window for support. His entire future seemed to balance on the edge of a blade. Tip one way and he and Charlie could make up the time they'd lost. Could start the life they'd always talked about together. Tip the other and his future with Socorro was secure. He'd continue his role as counterterrorism agent fighting the country's deadliest drug cartel and keep lives from being destroyed. But he couldn't have both. Not anymore.

"You didn't think I would do my own digging when I signed on with Socorro?" He'd done his homework on every operative under the Socorro umbrella. Cash and his determination to hide his brother's corruption from the DEA, Jocelyn and her drug addiction, Jones with his involvement in bringing down a state senator and Scarlett with her involvement in a military smuggling operation. He'd backed all of them up when they'd needed him, despite their dirty pasts and what had led them here, and now Socorro was going to make him choose between them and a woman he'd sworn to protect? Hell no.

"I know who your inside source is, Ivy. I know what he means to you, and that the only reason you're fighting this hard for closure is to get him out from under *Sangre por Sangre*'s control." Tendrils of resentment twisted in his chest.

"I would consider the next words out of your mouth very carefully, Morais." The investigator she'd once been—the one who refused to stop despite direct orders from her superiors, the concerns of her partner and the cost of her family—shifted back into place. "Because the only reason we knew about the cartel's interest in Charlie Acker is because of that source. Do you really want to put his life at risk for a woman who cost you your job with Homeland Security?"

She was right. If Socorro hadn't gotten to Charlie first, based off that intel, she'd be dead right now. He had no doubt about that. The fight drained out of him. Whether due to exhaustion or logic, Granger didn't know. He didn't care. He just wanted to protect the one thing in this world that made him feel needed. Human. "No. I want to know if you would be willing to ask the same thing of him that you're asking of Charlie."

"I already have, Granger." A softness he wasn't accustomed to seeing bled into Ivy's eyes. As though she'd expected a fight and was relieved they hadn't crossed that line. "The minute we realized *Sangre por Sangre* was a threat the Pentagon couldn't ignore, he chose the greater good over a future with me. And I let him. Because I knew a lot of innocent people would die if I didn't."

Socorro's founder walked away.

Chapter Ten

She could still taste him on her lips.

That perfect combination of peppermint toothpaste and something she could only describe as Granger. Citrus and earth battling for dominance and grounding. Her mouth tingled from the aftereffects, and Charlie couldn't help but press her fingers to the sensitive skin to hold onto that feeling a little bit longer.

Stinging pain erupted instead. She memorized the bruising shapes and scrapes along the backs of her hands, knowing where every single laceration and injury had originated. Her abductor felt as close to her in this room as he had in those woods despite her isolation, and Charlie knew deep down the scar of her survival would stay with her forever.

It'd been like that after the Alamo pipeline explosion. Her guilt, the physical pain, the grief of losing Sage had stuck with her until it'd gotten hard to breathe at times. But now she had something to help her fight back, to keep her grounded in the here and now. She hadn't even let herself cry for Erin yet. There just…hadn't been time.

The hospital room door swung open, centering Granger beneath the frame. Where he'd charged in earlier to be with her, he seemed sunken now. In his slow approach, in the way he didn't meet her gaze.

Tension bled into her shoulders. "Something happened. What is it?"

She wasn't sure she could handle anymore. All she'd wanted to do was figure out exactly what'd happened to Erin, and they were nowhere closer to attaining that answer. Instead, she'd uncovered a plot on the state capitol, the involvement of a drug cartel and suffered through an abduction. Then again, if she'd learned one thing from her childhood, it would be that anything worthwhile was worth standing your ground for. And giving Erin justice was worthwhile.

"We have your father in custody," Granger said. "Along with three cartel members."

Air caught in her throat. Very few things could surprise her anymore, and yet Granger stood there as though the arrest of Henry Acker didn't call for some kind of celebration. This was what they'd wanted, what they'd worked for. Understanding bled through the haze of pain and ibuprofen. Though was a private military contractor allowed to arrest terrorists? Or did they have to call in the feds to take over? Either way, Henry Acker wouldn't talk. Not until it benefited him at least. "I take it from the fact you're not saying that with a smile that he's made conditions Socorro isn't willing to meet."

He rounded the end of the bed, keeping his distance, and collapsed into a chair on the other side of the room. Mere minutes ago, he'd brought the past back with a single kiss. Now it felt as though he wasn't allowing himself to come close. What had changed since then? "We're private military contractors. We have no authority to arrest him. Even if we did, we don't have any physical evidence linking him to what happened to you, your sister's death or any attacks he's suspected of carrying out."

"You have me." Didn't he understand that? A sliver of panic worked to get the best of her, to undermine every second she'd stood up to her father. Henry Acker wasn't the kind of man to take an arrest lightly. Socorro would be added to his list of grievances and would be a continuous target of Acker's Army from here on out, and now he knew of her involvement with them. What did that mean for her? Erin had been held against her will all these years, never able to leave for fear their father would make her pay. What punishment awaited for the daughter who'd managed to escape? "My account of that night. My testimony or statement or whatever you want to call it. I wrote it all down."

"You ran, Charlie. You convinced the US government you died in that attack. Anything you say now against Henry Acker won't be considered in court, and I don't work for Homeland Security anymore to back you up." An invisible hand seemed to choke his voice. "Everything that happened the night of the Alamo pipeline ten years ago can't be used against him. No prosecutor will touch the case if you're involved, and we have nothing to hand over to the local authorities."

No. That wasn't how this was supposed to work. They'd had a plan. They were going to make her father pay for what he'd done. For the death of her oldest sister and the innocent lives of those four other bystanders. But she'd run. She'd given into her fear that no matter which path she took—to return to Vaughn or return to Granger—she'd be the one to suffer. And so she'd made her own choice. She'd wasted so much time being scared, and now Henry Acker would never answer for the nightmares that haunted her each night.

Acceptance never came easy. Not for her. But she had to fix this. She had to make this right. "Socorro wants to know about the deal my father made with *Sangre por Sangre* and what the cartel is planning to do. My guess is he isn't talking. What are his conditions?"

Granger leaned forward, bracing his elbows against his knees. "He'll only talk to you."

"Right." She didn't know what to say to that, what to think. Confronting her father face-to-face—without the threat of his soldiers or her sisters as a buffer, without an escape plan in mind—went against everything she believed. Henry Acker was a dangerous man to many. But more specifically to the people he claimed to care about. "Where is he being held?"

"In one of our interrogation rooms on the first floor." Granger shoved to stand despite the injuries he'd sustained fighting for their lives. Warmth skirted up her arm as he secured his hand in hers. "I asked you to get intel on your father and his organization once, and it was a mistake. I made you believe all I cared about was bringing him down, that I was sleeping with you only because you could help me secure an arrest. I can't ask you to go through that again."

"You mean sleep with you? I mean, it wasn't all that bad. There were a couple times I had to fake it, but who doesn't when they're focused on impressing a handsome federal agent instead of the actual experience?" Her attempt to lighten the mood pulled one corner of his mouth upward. Charlie squeezed his hand, taking in the battered skin over his knuckles and the blisters along his forearm. Blisters like the ones that'd left scars on her forearms.

Her stomach dropped at the realization she'd come close to losing the only person who'd ever given her permission to be herself. Not the soldier her father had reared. Not a fugitive on the run. Just…her. "Granger, the whole reason I agreed to be your CI was to stop my father from doing something terrible. I still believe in that cause. I just lost sight of it for a while, but these past couple days have reminded me of what's at stake if I keep running. And I don't want to keep being the kind of person who had a chance to save lives and chose to look the other way."

"You're not that person." Granger crouched beside the bed, leveling his gaze with hers.

"I was. All those years of hiding, of pretending I was dead. I could've done something. Maybe then those families would've gotten the closure they deserve instead of being constantly reminded their loved ones aren't there to celebrate birthdays, and Christmases and anniversaries with them." Charlie pulled her hand from his and threw back the covers. The sight of her bruised legs gave her pause, but she'd reached the tipping point. The victims of her father's attacks deserved better than monthly cash payments as a sorry excuse for an apology. They deserved justice, and she was going to give it to them. No matter what it cost her. Because living with this feeling of corruption and defectiveness wasn't a way to live. And she couldn't take the weight of surviving anymore. "They're still wondering what happened. Because of me."

"What are you doing?" Granger shot from his crouch by the bed and rounded to the other side. Strong hands held onto her as she tried setting her weight on her own two feet. A headache reared its ugly head while the bullet graze in her calf threatened to rip her balance from her, but she held onto him. "You're in no shape to talk to him now."

"We don't have a choice." She braced herself against him with one hand and grabbed for a pair of scrubs Dr. Piel had left for her to change into from the side table. "If *Sangre por Sangre* is planning something with my father's help, we need that information now. Not after it's too late."

She raised her gaze to his, a ridiculous amount of height between the two of them, but while Granger was trained and honed for the single purpose of accomplishing his mission, he didn't intimidate her. Quite the opposite. He was the anchor to keep her from getting lost in the storm. Charlie fought the bone-deep pain in her side, raising one hand to his face. The coarse hair along his jaw pricked at her skin and elicited a reaction from her nervous system. The bruising along his temple had darkened significantly, but there didn't seem to be any permanent damage. She could do this. She could do anything with him as her partner. Hadn't they already proven that? They were always better together. "I know how to make my father talk. I need you to trust me."

A hint of acceptance softened the corners of his eyes. "All right. What do you need from me?"

"Can you just...hold me up while I try to get dressed?" She leaned into him—physically, mentally, emotionally—as they worked together to replace the hospital gown with a fresh set of scrubs. Charlie tried to brush her hair out of her face, suddenly conscious of the fact she hadn't undressed in front of a man for ten years. "Was that as painful for you as it was for me?"

His laugh escaped as a short bark. "You have no idea."

She couldn't stop her responding smile. Only it didn't last. "I've been so focused on coming home, Erin's death and just not dying, I didn't think to ask if...this mess is keeping you from whomever you have waiting at home." Nervous energy charged through her. She had no right to ask about his personal life. She'd given that up ten years ago when she'd cut herself off from him, but the words were there all the same. Tainted with hope and a little bit of desperation. "Though I'm hoping the kiss earlier was a good indication. If not, I hope she kills you and hides the body so not even Zeus can find it."

Granger stared down at her, his hands on both her hips. Whether to keep her balanced or because he felt the same overwhelming need for physical contact that she did, Charlie didn't know. "I'm not involved with anyone."

"Were you?" She couldn't force herself to look at him, to expose the answer she needed to hear, but it was cycling through her, out of control. "Ten years is a long time. I would understand if moving on with your life meant moving on with someone else. Forgetting about me."

"I tried to forget about you. Several times with several different women." Granger slipped his index finger beneath her chin, nudging her to look up at him. Her insides unraveled under his study. "But I'm only going to say this once, Charlie."

Her brain latched onto every shift of his expression, ready to disengage at a moment's notice. To protect herself from the rejection and the hurt.

"Nobody wanted to date me," he said. "Because I was still in love with you."

HE HELD ONTO her as they navigated through the oversized maze of the building.

"Black tile, black walls." Charlie managed one slow step at a time. Brain injury had the ability to drop a person without provocation, not to mention a bullet to the calf, and he wasn't willing to push her harder than necessary to talk to the son of a bitch who'd given up his daughters for a chance to show his patriotism. "This entire building is ready for a funeral."

"Easier to clean up the blood we track in," he said.

Her smile told him she wasn't convinced, but there was a hint of truth to his answer. Socorro operatives charged into situations and engaged with threats that the US government couldn't or wouldn't risk anyone else for. That level of freedom and training came with costs. Mostly physical. Sometimes psychological.

They approached the elevator, and he hit the call button to take them down to the first floor. The shiny doors reflected their images. Her at his side, him ready to give his last breath for her. It was easy to imagine the years rolling by, of them as partners rather than resources for one another. The only one missing was Zeus. And he'd most likely gotten into another package of cookies while Granger paced the recovery wing. "You never told me what you've been doing while you were on the run. I'm guessing Charlie Acker hasn't been your name for a long time."

The doors parted, and Granger helped her into the car.

"No. It wasn't." She stared at the LED lights indicating the floor. "Living off the grid isn't as romantic as it sounds. The night of the Alamo pipeline explosion, I went back to Vaughn. I got the money I'd been saving for years between jobs around town and the cash you'd given me for intel—nearly ten thousand dollars—and I took off in one of the neighbor's cars."

The elevator dropped, and Granger's stomach shot higher in his torso. "I remember. The neighbor reported it stolen. I found that car outside of Boulder City, Nevada, two days later. Wiped clean. Couldn't prove you'd been the one to take it though."

"What good is all this survival information in my head unless I use it?" She pressed her temple to his arm as the descending numbers on the LED screen lit up. "I spent the first few years stockpiling safe houses. Food, water, money, weapons, ammunition. I moved from place to place and switched up my car every time I stopped. Sooner than I expected, I ran out of money. I had to start working. Just here and there. Nothing permanent, and nothing that required a background check."

"I take it you're well-versed in breakfast foods then." The elevator pinged with their arrival, and the doors parted. He helped her over the threshold onto the first floor, doing everything in his power not to look at the spot where he'd nearly bled out from the gunshot wound three weeks ago. His shoulder was still sore, but putting eyes on where it'd happened intensified the pain. Granger didn't come down to this level, and if he did, he was sure to take the stairs on the other side of the building. His shoulder seemed to sense his proximity to the garage, as it had two days ago. Trauma was a given in his line of work, but ignoring the aftereffects would tear him apart from the inside if he let it.

"I might be. Maybe one of these days, you'll find out." Charlie's voice faded the longer he directed his attention to holding back the memories. "Granger?"

He rolled his shoulder back to counter the ache spreading down his arm. Damn it, his fingers were tingling. Going numb. He'd managed to keep himself in check since retreating back to Socorro by focusing on Charlie's needs, but his brain wasn't going to let him replace one gunfight with another and have him walk away unscathed. "Is that what you dug up at your safehouse the other day? Another cache you'd hidden?"

The attempt to focus himself failed.

Charlie centered herself in his vision. Brown eyes locked on him and refused to let him go. She followed him as he tried to turn away. "Granger, look at me. What's going on?"

"It's nothing." He shook his head, as though the simple action could erase the pressure building in his head. "The interrogation room is this way."

"I'm not going anywhere until you tell me what just

happened." With one hand latched onto his arm, she hit the elevator call button just as the doors closed. "That asshole in Vaughn hit you pretty hard. Are you dizzy, nauseous? Dr. Piel said you guys come in here all the time with head injuries. She should take a look."

His pulse pounded hard behind his ears. Too hard. He closed his eyes, at the mercy of his own mind. The last place he wanted to be. "Keep talking. I just...need to focus on something else."

"Okay." Charlie slid one hand along his shoulder as the elevator doors tried to close on them, and the pain seemed to recede with her touch. Which he knew was impossible. Physical contact didn't change the sensitivity of pain receptors, but her touch was the distraction he needed. "Do you remember the night we met? How I almost shot you for walking onto my father's property uninvited? I was in the backyard skinning the jackrabbits I'd shot that day. My rifle was right there, yet you walked straight up to me with your hands up. I was ready to pull the trigger, but you said the one thing that convinced me to put down the rifle."

He gritted through the crushing loss of control determined to get the best of him. "I asked if you wanted some strawberry ice cream."

"It sounded so ridiculous." She smoothed circles into the back of his shoulder. Right where he needed her. "You told me you'd stopped into a diner on the way to Vaughn and ordered a strawberry shake, but they'd accidentally given you two. And you offered me one. Handed it to me and everything, and all I could think to myself was it was a good thing you'd come to me, because anyone else would've shot a stranger dead on the spot so late at night. Little did I know you'd been watching me for weeks by then."

The pressure in his head was draining with every word from her sweet mouth. Keeping him in the here and now, tethering him to reality. He wasn't back in the garage. He wasn't the only one standing between his fellow operatives and the *Sangre por Sangre* cartel. Charlie was there too. "I knew you liked strawberry milkshakes."

"They're still my favorite. Though I wasn't able to find anything that compared to the one you gave me that night. Then again, maybe it wasn't the shake I remember the most." Charlie's fingers dipped under the collar of his shirt, smoothing her fingers directly against the rise of scar tissue on the back of his left shoulder. Right where the bullet had been surgically removed. "Dr. Piel said that Socorro operatives have a dangerous job. I asked if you'd been to see for her anything other than a head injury in the past. She refused to tell me, but I'm guessing this isn't a scar from when you had the chicken pox as a kid."

Her other hand fanned the front of his collarbone, and Granger couldn't help but straighten. He grabbed for her hand, afraid of what she'd find beneath his shirt. "Charlie."

She slipped her hand out of his, using only her fingertips to study the healing wound, and suddenly it felt like she was the one holding him up. Her inhale hissed in his ear. "Smaller in the front, bigger in the back. Long distance. Fresh. No more than a few weeks old from the pliability of the surrounding tissue. But the exit wound feels...surgical. Not like a normal gunshot wound. Dr. Piel was able to remove the bullet?"

"Most of it," he said.

Charlie pressed herself into his arms, searching the floor. What she saw or what she expected to see, he didn't know. "You were shot. Here?"

He could breathe now. Odd. Memories from the past took longer for him to recover from, but there was something about Charlie—the way she seemed to center him and unbalance him all at the same time—that cut through the fear following him everywhere he went. "In the garage. I bled out here. We were under attack. I was the only one keeping them from penetrating the upper floors."

"Sangre por Sangre." Setting her forehead against his jaw, she held onto him. "Why don't you want me to see it?"

"Because then you'll finally see what kind of man I am." His mouth dried. "That I wasn't strong enough to protect you ten years ago, and that I might not be strong enough to shield you from what's coming now."

Charlie pulled back. The overhead lights were much brighter here, accentuating the bruise patterns, cuts and blood across her beautiful skin. Her broken nose. She pressed her finger over his heart. "I know exactly what kind of man you are, Granger Morais. You're the kind of man who runs into a fight that isn't yours to begin with. You have a hard time trusting people, but once you do, that trust lasts a lifetime, even when the person on the receiving end doesn't deserve it. You're committed and reliable and the only person who has ever considered what's best for me instead of exerting your power over me like everyone else. And nothing—not a bullet wound or any other injuries—is going to convince me you aren't the man I want at my side for what comes next. Your dog can come too. I'm sure we can bring snacks or—"

Granger crushed his mouth to hers. The last of his uncertainty fled, and he fed off the strength she'd lent him. He had survived the past three weeks on a mixture of adrenaline and duty, and for the first time since he'd come out of Dr. Piel's operating suite, he was beginning to feel whole. Duty wouldn't keep him moving forward. He had to have a hand in his own future. One of his own design. It was up to him. "Have you been practicing that speech?"

"Maybe a little." She smiled, kissing him again. Charlie intertwined her fingers with his, and it was as though they hadn't missed a step in the past ten years. "I have a few speeches on hand. Most of them are rewritten arguments I've had with my sisters, so I'm the one who wins."

Granger caught sight of Ivy at the end of the corridor. Waiting. "You got one of those for your father?"

She angled away from him, and her smile fell. This was it. What the past decade of her living on the run and faking her death had built to: giving those she'd hurt the justice they deserved. And Granger couldn't help but admire her strength. "No, but I'm sure I'll think of something along the way."

Chapter Eleven

Charlie didn't look back as she slipped through the door to the interrogation room. The man inside looked up at her, as though he'd expected Socorro to play into his hands all along. Knowing her father, his love of strategy and his ability to manipulate even the most seasoned preppers, she was probably right. "Dad."

"You came." His white-gray hair seemed to glow under the reflection of the overhead lights, aging him ten years if she didn't know any better. The lines spidering away from his eyes and mouth seemed deeper than even twenty-four hours ago, and she couldn't help but note the tension in his hands as he pulled against the cuffs securing him to a solid metal ring embedded in the table.

"Did I have any other choice?" Charlie forced herself to take a step forward, all too aware of the pressure of Granger's attention from the other side of the one-way glass. And he wasn't alone.

The interrogation room was exactly as she'd imagined. Though the ones she'd seen in her binge of movies and television she'd never been allowed to watch growing up came across grimier than this. If she'd stuck around after the attack at the pipeline, she might've gotten to see one herself.

Though Granger had told her he didn't actually have the authority to hold her father on charges, she couldn't help but wonder what would happen to him after their conversation. Would they let her father go back to Vaughn? Or would Socorro hold him indefinitely in the interest of public safety?

She pulled out the chair opposite her father and took a seat, unable to think of the last time they'd been alone together. Not as one of his soldiers waiting for their next mission assignment. As father and daughter. Charlie locked her jaw against the pain flaring in her legs and torso. The bruises on her hands were darker now. Impossible to ignore. "That woman, Ivy, said you wouldn't talk to anyone but me."

"I don't trust them." He set his cuffed wrists against the table, the metallic scratch of stainless steel on steel louder than expected.

"But you trust me?" she asked.

Henry Acker shut down any hint of what was going on in his head, pulling away from the table. His hands disappeared into his lap, the chain between the cuffs pulling tight. "I know they're listening. Watching us from the other side of the glass. Recording us too."

He nodded toward the camera installed in the corner of the room. The red light beneath the lens said he was right. She stared into the glass, unafraid of exposure now. It was a bittersweet feeling, contradictory to the way she'd lived her life these past ten years. There wasn't any more fear. Because she had a promise from a former counterterrorism agent that nothing would hurt her again, and she believed him.

"They want to know about the deal you made with *Sangre por Sangre*. And after fighting against a cartel member for my life, so do I." Because all of this—Erin's death, her own abduction, nearly losing Granger in that fire—could all be linked back to the man sitting across from her. Running hadn't changed anything. He was still the father who kept his emotional distance and favored punishment and duty over the stability she'd needed all her life. And she'd been a fool to think anything would change when faced with the consequences of his choices.

"I can't tell you about that," he said. "Not yet."

"Of course not. Because everything needs to be on your terms, doesn't it? What time I woke up and went to sleep, what I ate, how many hours I spent shooting, how I spent my free time, who I talked to, who I was allowed to date." She couldn't hold back the humorless laugh as the anger burned. Charlie stretched her interlaced hands across the table and shoved to her feet. Though not without a shot of pain in her calf. "Can you blame me for running when I had a shot at freedom?"

"It was for your own good." He notched that proud chin of his higher. Every ounce the man who'd molded her into exactly what he wanted her to be. "Everything I did, I did to protect you. To make sure you could protect yourself when the fight came to Vaughn."

"What fight, Dad? The people you hate so much haven't stepped foot in Vaughn since the night of mom's death. And from where I'm standing, you've brought this mess to your own door by making a deal with a drug cartel." She couldn't be in this room anymore. Not with him. Not ever again. "I can't believe I even came in here expecting a real conversation with you. You've never seen me as anything more than something to control. Me, Sage and Erin. We weren't your daughters. We were tools to be used for your own agenda, nothing more, and that makes you a real son of a bitch."

She turned to leave. For the last time.

"I couldn't lose you too." His voice warbled from behind. So unlike the man she'd feared growing up. "I couldn't lose any of you. You and your sisters."

Charlie had almost made it to the door with every intention of stepping through it and telling Socorro's founder to do whatever she saw fit with her father. But something in the way his voice crumbled held her still. "What are you talking about?"

"After your mother… I couldn't stand the thought of losing you the way I lost her." He flattened his palms on the table, staring down at them as though he didn't recognize his own hands. "I needed you to be stronger than she was."

A knot twisted in Charlie's gut. "Stronger how?"

"Your mother wasn't killed by police officers searching for a fugitive. I know what I told you girls, but she wasn't keeping them from searching the house. There was no struggle that led to her getting shot. She *left*, Charlie," he said. "She abandoned us."

What? She countered her retreat as a simmering heat spread under her skin, and her father seemed to melt right in his chair. "You're lying. You said we had to stay vigilant. That Acker's Army would protect our family and friends from a government that didn't care about who it hurt to get what it wanted. I believed you. For a long time, I believed you."

His voice barely reached over the thud of her pulse behind her ears. "I lied. To you and Sage and Erin."

A hot combination of fear and uncertainty urged her to leave, to put everything about the past few minutes behind her, but the thought of fear running her life a second longer held her in place. Bringing her hand to her mouth, she tried to stop the surge of acid as her entire life came apart. "Her headstone is in the backyard of your property. We had a funeral."

"You're right. I had it made when I realized she wasn't coming back. I just couldn't tell you girls the truth. I didn't want you to have to face the fact she left you behind." Her father tried to push away from the table, but the cuffs protested. "Before you were old enough to remember, I lost my job, then our house, our savings and everything else we owned. We had nowhere else to go. Vaughn seemed like a place to start over. Do things differently. But your mother was miserable from the moment we stepped foot in that house. She begged me to leave, but we couldn't go back. Every day I dug my heels in, the heavier her expression got. Until I didn't recognize her anymore. By the time I realized what I'd done, it was too late. She was gone. She'd packed her things and left in the middle of the night. Suddenly, I had three girls asking me where their mother was, and I didn't have any answers. I couldn't give you three answers."

Charlie didn't know what to believe. Everything she'd known about her father—why she'd been forced to adhere to his rules and commands, why she'd had to learn to protect herself—was a lie. "You could've told us the truth. We could've handled it. Instead, you raised us to believe our own government was responsible for killing our mother. You turned us into extremists willing to participate in your delusions. You lied to us about keeping the rest of our family safe. And for what, Dad? Why would you put us through all of that? Why would you carry out those attacks if you didn't really believe in what you were fighting for?"

"I did believe, damn it." The words were ground out through clenched teeth. He'd lost control, and for the first time in…ever, Charlie got a glimpse of a man who might be as human as she was. "My job, our house, our savings—all of it was taken by this government, Charlie. They laid off thousands during the economic crash. They took everything from us, and I couldn't let it go. I was bitter and angry and afraid we'd never recover." Her father sat back in his chair, trying to get his breathing level. "The night your mother left, we fought. She told me that at some point I had to stop being a victim. I had to step up and be a man and take care of my family. So that's what I did."

Charlie stood a bit straighter. Not really sure what to say to that, how to respond to the first hint of fear from a man who didn't seem to be scared of anything.

"That singular focus was the only sense of purpose I had." Her father's voice grew stronger. "We were forced to move to Vaughn out of desperation, but I did what was best for my family. I taught myself how to grow vegetables, preserve the harvest, how to shoot, hunt, survive the wilderness, if need be. I stockpiled supplies, weapons and ammunition to defend what little we had. The local church helped keep our bellies full, and I made sure to serve anywhere in the community I could for extra help. People appreciated it. Started seeking me out for advice on how to support their own families. That advice spread, and within a few years of us arriving, Vaughn had become a stronghold against the outside world. One I wasn't willing to risk losing. So yes, I recruited fighters willing to protect what was ours, and I built my girls to be stronger than their mother—stronger than me—and look at you now."

His rant had ended, leaving Charlie empty and cold and more confused than when she'd walked into this room.

"Yeah. Look at me now. Look at Sage and Erin." She didn't know whether to believe him or not. Or if he was manipulating her to get what he wanted from her again. "Those little girls you promised to protect? We didn't want to be soldiers or answer to a general. We just wanted our father. To know that he loved us, and you failed. They're *dead*, Dad. Because of you. And I'm next unless you tell me about the deal you made with *Sangre por Sangre*."

"Don't you dare try to put Sage's death on me, Charlie Grace Acker. Had you followed through with your mission, she would still be alive, but you got involved with that federal agent out there and ran. Like a coward." Henry Acker pulled his shoulders back, sinking into his chair. Calm. Collected. "As for what happened to Erin, you don't have to worry about that. I've already taken care of it."

GRANGER WAS AT the door before Charlie could manage to pull it open.

Every cell in his body honed in on the despair in her eyes and wanted to assure her that anything out of Henry Acker's mouth couldn't be trusted. "Tell me what's going through your head."

She let the door close behind her, folding her arms across her chest. The motion set off a flinch in her expression. Whatever Dr. Piel had given her to counteract the pain was wearing thin. "I don't know what to think. My entire life my father told me one version of events, and now... I don't know what to believe. Except that I'm hungry."

"I can help with that." Granger pulled her into his arms, ready to be anything she needed in that moment. Support, a chef, someone to work through Acker's motives with. "I think Jocelyn just added some lasagna to the fridge. That is if Zeus hasn't already gotten to it. He's like Garfield the cat, except he doesn't know when he's full."

"Do you have any insight into *Sangre por Sangre*'s plan to attack the state capitol, or how they'll try to regain their standing?" Ivy Bardot had a job to do, and she wasn't wasting anytime in doing it, despite the obvious exhaustion in Charlie's face. "Anything actionable we can use?"

Granger tightened his hold on Charlie. She could only take so much before she crashed from what'd happened over the past couple days. She was running on empty with demands coming from every angle, and a second interrogation sure as hell wasn't going to make things any better.

"No, but I'm fairly positive he didn't have anything to do with Erin's death. The man who took me from Vaughn. He said something about my sister not fighting back as much as I had. My father is many things, but with what he's told me about his reasons for building Acker's Army, it's hard to imagine he would do anything to hurt the family he was so scared of losing." Charlie hugged herself, swaying on her feet. "Something is keeping him from telling us about the deal he made with the cartel. I'm not sure what it is, but you heard him. My father isn't the kind of man to take anything lying down. He's not afraid to stand up for what he believes or fight against a bigger and stronger opponent if it means keeping what he has. My guess? *Sangre por Sangre* is holding something over his head to ensure his cooperation and support."

"We know of three attacks that could potentially be linked to Henry Acker. He's thorough and strategic and, according to his history, has every reason to want *Sangre por Sangre* to succeed." Ivy stared into the interrogation room from behind the one-way glass. "What could a man like him possibly fear losing?"

Charlie's shoulders raised on a strong inhale. "I think he's afraid of losing me. When I mentioned that Sage and Erin were dead, and that I'm next, he reacted."

"I didn't see anything." Granger studied the man on the other side of the glass, looking for something— anything—that would give him an idea of what was coming.

"When you grow up in a culture of being prepared at all times and where mistakes are more deadly than the words you say, you learn to predict and read people's emotions in the smallest ways. You wouldn't have seen it, but the muscles on the left side of his jaw flexed. He was biting down," she said.

"Let's say you're right." Ivy faced them. "*Sangre por Sangre* can destroy your father with something in their possession, and they're using it to force his compliance. Maybe it's proof he and his army are involved in attacks like the Alamo pipeline. What kind of support would your father be able to provide to the cartel?"

"Weapons. Manpower. Supplies." Exhaustion played out in Charlie's eyes, to the point Granger wasn't sure how much longer she would be able to stand. She was pushing herself, driving harder than she needed, because this was how she believed she could make up for her mistakes. The truth was she couldn't. Not really. The five lives that'd been taken the night of the pipeline attack were gone. And they were never coming back. Even if they managed to prove Henry Acker was at fault—that Charlie was just a pawn in his game—that guilt wouldn't go away. She wouldn't let it. "But explosives are his specialty. He's been stealing them from construction sites across the state for years. Primarily C4. Sometimes dynamite. Nothing that could alert the ATF or tie back to him."

"That was why Homeland Security was never able to pinpoint where the C4 used in the Alamo pipeline attack came from." Granger should've known, but without alerts raised from those construction sites, he and the rest of his team had been operating blind. "That's how Acker kept under the radar."

Charlie set her hand against his forearm. "I'm sorry. I wanted to tell you, but…"

"You were the one tasked with getting your hands on the explosives." Hell. Did Henry Acker have no shame? Using his own daughter to commit felonies had kept him out of a federal prison, but at what cost? "If I had any proof of your involvement in the attack on the Alamo pipeline, not just that your blood was found at the scene, I would be forced to arrest you. You would be sentenced to federal prison for the rest of your life. Without parole."

A hint of fear etched into Charlie's features.

"Which is still a possibility, Ms. Acker. But considering your cooperation with this investigation, I'm sure I can put in a good word with Homeland Security when this is all over. Until then we'll assume *Sangre por Sangre* is in the market for explosives, which means their resources are still dwindling. That could work for us." Ivy Bardot brought their attention back to her. Time was running out. Whatever the cartel planned depended on Henry Acker, and without the support of Acker's Army, *Sangre por Sangre* might jump the gun. "I want eyes on the entire town of Vaughn. Acker might be stuck here, but that doesn't mean his subordinates aren't carrying out his orders as we speak. I'll send two operatives to keep us up-to-date. What about the blueprints you recovered from Acker's office?"

Granger's mind was already working through the snippets of handwriting he'd read on the thin paper in Henry Acker's office. He took out his phone and hit the photos app, bringing up the overhead view of Henry Acker's desk. "I got a clear photo of the notes, but they're unreadable. I don't know what the hell kind of language it's written is, but I've never seen it before."

He centered his phone between the three of them.

"It's a code." Ivy backed away, apparently not willing to waste her time trying to decipher it right then and there. "I've seen it before, years ago, but this one has been altered. My partner and I were assigned to a case of a young woman found murdered out in the middle of the desert, and this code was carved into her back. We weren't able to decipher its meaning before another woman was killed. We had a suspect that turned out to have a connection with an up-and-coming drug cartel called *Sangre por Sangre*. It was our first interaction with them."

"You think whoever made these notes might be involved in your original case?" Granger couldn't convince himself this was nothing more than a coincidence. "Did you make an arrest?"

"We were closing in, but the suspect escaped," Ivy said. "My partner at the time determined it was unlikely he'd resurface as long as the FBI was on the hunt."

"So he went undercover in the cartel to find the killer. He's your source inside *Sangre por Sangre*, the one who gave us the heads up on the cartel's interest in Charlie." Socorro's founder's past was beginning to make sense, despite her determination to shut everyone out and focus on the one goal they could control. "And given he's still there, I take it your partner hasn't found what he's looking for."

"Not yet." Ivy slipped her hands into her slacks, seemingly at ease, but Granger knew better.

There was an added tension at the corner of the woman's mouth, and he realized Charlie had been right. Learning to read people's masking behavior under pressure took time and a skill he hadn't been aware he'd picked up around his superior.

"What about the code? Were you able to decipher its meaning?" A brightness Granger hadn't expected entered Charlie's voice. As though this was the lead they'd been waiting for.

"Yes. In the end, our analysts were able to determine the three-letter key that unlocked the entire phrase," Ivy said. "Unfortunately, it was too late to save another woman from turning up dead."

"Scarlett is good at this kind of stuff. She might be able to narrow down the key and get us the answers we need." Granger had already sent the blueprints to Socorro's security consultant, but the last time he'd checked in, she hadn't been able to give him an update. "What were the three letters used in your case to unlock the phrase?"

"B, A and P." Ivy cut her attention back to Henry Acker, who'd slowly gotten to his feet. He was trying to get out of his cuffs. "The letters themselves didn't produce anything significant, but there was a reason the killer chose them. We were just never able to determine his motive."

"There's another option," Charlie said. "We recovered the blueprints from my father's office, but the notes aren't written in his handwriting. If we're right that *Sangre por Sangre* is using my father and Acker's Army in their plan, it means he should be able to read those notes. We can just ask him."

"The problem is your father isn't talking." Granger couldn't stand the thought of her going back in there to face the fact Acker had lied to Charlie her entire life. And given her exhaustion and injuries, she couldn't physically interrogate Henry Acker again. "He's shut down every attempt we've made to get the cartel's plan."

Movement caught Granger's attention through the one-way glass, where Henry Acker was currently bending over the table toward his hands. The man reached into his mouth and withdrew a thin rectangular piece of metal. "He's got a blade!"

Granger maneuvered around Charlie, pulling her out of his way as he charged into the interrogation room. Henry Acker smiled as he brought the blade to his neck and pressed it through the skin of his neck. "Stop them."

Granger bolted across the table, but it was too late.

Henry Acker fell against the table as his wound pumped blood onto the floor.

Chapter Twelve

The blood was still pooled on the floor.

Charlie couldn't make herself look away. "I don't understand. He was...sitting right there. This doesn't make sense."

"It happened so fast." Granger's voice had lost its sense of control. "I tried to stop him. I'm so sorry, Charlie. I don't know how it happened."

She knew. She'd watched the whole thing as though the recording of her life had somehow caught in the VCR she'd grown up with and froze on the single frame of her father ending his life. And she'd just stood there. Unable to move or stop him. In that single moment, her father had ignored the mountain of muscle coming right at him, and he'd looked straight at her.

Stop them.

All this time, all these years, she'd known Henry Acker as a man of conviction. One who'd never given in to threats from law enforcement, who'd never stood down from a fight or showed an ounce of weakness. What had changed?

Dr. Piel zipped the body bag closed over her father's face as two other Socorro operatives wheeled the remains out on the stretcher. Because that was what he was now. The monster of a man she'd feared would swallow her up and systematically destroy her was nothing but a shell now. Sympathy smoothed the physician's expression as Dr. Piel followed the team out of the interrogation room. "Charlie, I'm very sorry for your loss."

"Thank you." A heaviness she couldn't describe closed in around her. A disconnect between her body and her brain. The events of the past three days were starting to compound. How much more was she expected to take? And why couldn't she look away from the blood on the floor? "I just…don't understand."

"Unfortunately, that's not uncommon. Family and friends rarely have answers when something like this occurs, but I'm happy to request his medical records if that will help." The doctor bounced her gaze to Granger and back. "What's important is that you take care of yourself right now. You're injured and running on fumes."

"I don't care." The tears were back, and she hated them. She hated that she still felt something for the man who'd turned her into…whatever it was he wanted her to be. She hated that he still had this control over her, that he could get her to grieve for him. And she hated that he'd taken his deal with the people who'd abducted her into that body bag with him.

"Charlie." Granger placed a supportive hand under her elbow. "Dr. Piel's right. You look like you're about to collapse. You need some sleep and a few thousand calories to help you recover."

"I don't want to sleep, and I don't want to eat. I want to know what he meant by what he said." She turned all that building anger onto the man who deserved it the least. It flooded through her, out of control. Her heart rate spiked. She couldn't breathe, couldn't think. The only thought in her mind was that last image of Henry Acker holding a razor blade to his neck. Over and over. She'd fed off her drive to stay one step ahead of her father for the past ten years, and now he just got to leave? That didn't seem fair. "Stop them. What the hell is that supposed to mean, Granger? I have spent my entire life following his commands and cleaning up his messes. And now I'm just expected to…what? Take down an entire cartel at his suggestion?"

A rush of dizziness threatened to take her down. Charlie stumbled back into the wall. Low voices warbled in and out as Granger and Dr. Piel reached for her. Her legs gave out, and she collapsed. There were others closing in on her. Too close. "He wasn't supposed to die."

"She's likely dehydrated. We need to get her to my exam room for an IV. Now." Dr. Piel shoved to stand as strong arms threaded behind Charlie's shoulders and along the backs of her knees. "Let's go."

"I've got you, Charlie. It's going to be okay." Granger held onto her, and she couldn't help but want to bury herself in his strength. Walls and overhead lights blurred as he somehow managed to run with her weight at a full sprint. No matter the threat or the injury, he refused to back down, and she needed that right now. She needed his innate belief that the things they'd sacrificed could actually make the world a better place, because she was losing her grip. "We're going to get through this."

Her body hurt. She was tired. She didn't want to do

this anymore. Every decision that'd led her to this point had been to get justice for the lives Henry Acker had ruined, but there was no justice to be had anymore. There was nothing she could do to give them closure. Except to make sure her father's deal with *Sangre por Sangre* never saw the light of day. "Put me down."

Her voice barely carried over the pound of her own pulse. Charlie held onto consciousness by a single thread as exhaustion pulled at her muscles and brain. Time seemed to slip by. Second by second, minute by minute, and she had no control over it. Her head ached, and she couldn't fight against the pull as her body tried to give up its fight.

Dr. Piel rushed ahead. "In here."

Maneuvering her headfirst through the door, Granger angled her down onto the examination table. Bright lights bleached Charlie's vision a split second before Granger centered himself over the source. "The doctor's just going to give you a saline drip. You're dehydrated and exhausted. You've got to give your body some time to recover."

"No." That single word slurred in her own ears. She tried to peel herself off the table, but Granger's hand held her in place. "I can't stay here."

Confusion deepened the three distinct lines between his brows. "Charlie, you can barely stand on your own."

"I don't care. I have to leave. Please let me leave." She fisted his shirt to haul herself upright.

"Granger, I need you to hold her still, or I'm going to puncture something I'm not supposed to." Dr. Piel moved in close. Stinging pain pricked at the soft skin of Charlie's inner elbow.

Her fight-or-flight kicked in. She ripped her arm back, tearing free of whatever the doctor had stabbed her with. Momentum forced her to overcorrect. The exam room blurred, and she hit the floor on the other side of the table. Adrenaline surged hot and fast. It replaced the pain spiking along her calf, and she managed to get to her feet.

"Charlie." Granger moved to intercept her, but the doctor held a hand against his chest.

"Don't, Granger. Give her space. She's not thinking clearly," Dr. Piel said. "Charlie, why do you need to leave?"

A massive migraine spread from the base of her skull. Charlie dared a step forward. Then another. She was capable of ordering her limbs to follow her commands, but something didn't feel right. A numbness had taken hold. Not just in her body, but her mind. Using the end of the exam table to steady herself, Charlie took in the concern etched into Granger's face. "Because my father was right. I'm the only one who can stop *Sangre por Sangre.*"

"I told you before. You're not in this alone. I know it feels that way, but it's not true." He raised his hands out in front of him, as though approaching a wild animal, and maybe he was right to do so. Maybe Granger should think about himself first for once. "Every operative in this place will do whatever it takes to make sure the cartel never regains power. Especially me."

He wasn't going to let her go. That was clear now,

and the tears burned down her face. Walking away from him had been the hardest decision she'd ever made in her life. Not becoming his CI. Not choosing to betray her father and everything he believed in. But leaving Granger behind. Because she'd been in love with him. Was still in love with him.

She wasn't sure why it'd taken her so long to realize that was the reason she'd survived her abduction. Something deep inside of her had wanted what they'd had back enough to fight for her life when the chances of surviving were the lowest. It'd been the possibility of being in his orbit that had driven her to attack the driver of a vehicle exceeding sixty miles an hour in the middle of the desert with no concern for the consequences. All she'd wanted these past ten years was to feel him again, to know she wasn't alone.

And she had to save that.

Because the longer he sided with her in this battle, the higher chance she'd lose him all over again. They'd come too close to death. He wouldn't survive the next time. She felt that truth in through the numbness, deep down into her bones.

So she had to hurt him. She had to make him see the truth. That there wouldn't be a future for them as long as she kept running. Was that what her father had been trying to tell her?

Charlie spotted an array of surgical tools on a rolling cart a few feet away. She darted for the scalpel, and both Granger and Dr. Piel backed up. There was only one way out of this, and damn it, he was going to force her to use it. She recalled the turns they'd taken to get to this room despite the fog working to shut down her cognitive function. She had to go. Now. "Let me leave, Granger."

"Why?" Understanding seemed to hit, and his expression crumbled right in front of her. Granger lowered his hands, facing off with her as he had the night they'd met. "Why are you doing this? After everything we've been through together, why can't you trust me?"

Her hand shook around the scalpel. Four words formed in her mind, and it took everything in her power to force them out. "That's the first lesson they teach you in Acker's Army, Agent Morais. I don't trust anyone."

Charlie rounded the end of the exam table and headed for the door. Without so much as a glance backward, she ran.

GRANGER STARED AFTER HER.

"I can alert Scarlett. She can use the security system to shut down the building." Dr. Piel lunged for the phone at the desk shoved into the corner of the exam room. Raising the handset to her ear, she hit one of the buttons. "Charlie isn't going to make it far. She's—"

A tearing Granger had become all too familiar with clawed through his chest. It had nothing to do with the shrapnel in his shoulder and everything to do with the woman who'd left him behind. Again. "Let her go."

"We can stop her." Dr. Piel turned to face him. "She needs medical attention. If she doesn't get fluids, she might experience seizures, swelling in her brain and possibly lapse into a coma."

"Hang up the phone. Alerting security won't do any

good." Granger headed for the door. "It doesn't matter how far she gets. We can't keep her here against her will."

"You survived a forest fire to find her," Dr. Piel said. "You risked your own life to pull her out of that burning vehicle. She just watched her father kill himself. She's obviously not in her right mind, and you're just going to let her go out there alone? *Sangre por Sangre* will find her, Granger. Doesn't that concern you?"

Granger didn't bother turning back. He'd spent years trying to locate a woman who didn't want to be found. And damn it, he was tired of the chase. He had a job to do: stop *Sangre por Sangre* from regaining their broken power. "Charlie made her choice."

Working through the maze of Socorro's headquarters, he made it to his bedroom and shoved inside. Zeus bounced off the bed and approached the door. Waiting. "She's not coming."

Granger unlocked the gun safe, pulling a weapon from inside. Acker's Army had taken his preferred sidearm, and there was a chance he was never going to get it back. He grabbed a few more pieces of gear and ammunition, including his Kevlar vest, and rammed it into one of the duffel bags he pulled from under the bed. The zipper scratched at the scabs along the back of his hand, tearing a hardened chunk of skin free. Blood dripped down his wrist, but he didn't have the patience to bandage the wound.

Sangre por Sangre had attempted to build an underground headquarters on twenty-two acres of land owned by one of its lieutenants, now long dead. There wasn't much of the building left after one of Socorro's operatives had literally torn the place down searching for the woman he loved after her abduction, but Granger couldn't think of a more fitting safe house for the few remaining members of the cartel. Off the grid, decommissioned and too dangerous to occupy.

He'd start there.

A trail of dust cut across his window. Granger straightened, watching as one of Socorro's SUV's sped across the New Mexican landscape, heading east. The entire team was grounded from assignments until the details of Henry Acker's death could be related to the local police. Which meant the driver was Charlie.

Granger shouldered his gear.

The bull terrier didn't seem to get the message Charlie wasn't going to walk through that door and grace Zeus with her presence. "Come on. We've got an assignment."

The K9 didn't budge.

"Zeus." The call came out harsher than Granger meant it to, and the dog turned on him with a whine. His heart—finally starting to piece itself back together these past few days—fractured at the sight of Zeus's sadness. He slipped the duffel strap off and let the bag hit the floor, lowering himself to the K9's level. "I know. I'm going to miss her too."

Granger allowed himself this moment of peace. Of him and Zeus hurting for the same loss. In a matter of days, Charlie had slipped back into his life and upended his world all over again. He didn't know how, and hell, it didn't really matter. Because there was no going back. "Come on, bud. We've got some cartel members to sit on."

But the truth was, he just felt tired. And watching Charlie leave hurt more than the bullet shard in his shoulder, except this one had gone straight through his heart. He was bloody knuckled, battered and bruised. Because of her. Because of his need to keep her in a life she never intended to stay in. It seemed no matter what choice he made or how he tried to make up for failing Charlie in the past, he would always be second best.

To her need for freedom.

Her need for justice.

And her need to prove herself as an individual rather than a soldier.

Granger collected his bag and headed for the door. Only to be stopped by the journal sitting on the edge of his bed. Erin Acker's journal. Charlie had broken into her father's house for it, risked her life for it. It didn't seem right to leave it here. He slipped it into one of the side pockets of his duffel and hit the hallway with Zeus on his heels. He took the stairs, uninterested in becoming another victim to the dark images and pressure in his head waiting to ambush him on the first floor. He mentally worked through the layout of *Sangre por Sangre*'s battered headquarters as he entered Socorro's garage.

To find Ivy Bardot standing in front of his SUV.

Understanding hit. "You gave her the keys and let her leave." Granger should've known. All this time, he'd wondered if his superior allowed herself to consider anything but the mission. Now he had his answer.

Socorro's founder didn't bother denying it. "You know

as well as I do she's the key to the cartel's entire plan. There's something about her that *Sangre por Sangre* wants, and we need to know what that something is."

"So you gave her an SUV and sent her on her way." Son of a bitch. Ivy was going to use Charlie as bait. "You want her to lead us straight to the cartel."

"Wouldn't you have done the same in my position?" she asked.

Rage exploded through his chest and shot up his throat. Granger closed the distance between them as the last of his control slipped away. "I would've taken one look at her and realized she isn't ready for the fight she's walking into."

Ivy stared up at him, so damn calm. She wasn't the least bit intimidated by a man twice her size. She knew as well as he did she could put him on his ass faster than he could process the threat, and she wasn't afraid to prove it at the slightest provocation. "And yet you didn't stop her when she ran from Dr. Piel's exam room."

The accusation neutralized the fire in his veins, but it wasn't strong enough to quiet the concern pushing him to act. He wasn't strong enough. Charlie was gunning for a fight she wouldn't win alone, and there was nothing he could do to convince her otherwise. The night of the Alamo pipeline attack, he'd felt useless. Wondering where he'd gone wrong and how he could've changed the course of events. Losing his job at Homeland Security as a consequence of defying orders to let Charlie loose as his CI had only shored up that crack in his confidence.

This was worse.

She'd been right there, within reach, and he'd somehow lost her all over again. Granger tightened his hold on his gear. "You brought me into Socorro because I know the way terrorist organizations and the members inside them work. *Sangre por Sangre* might not fit the bill exactly, but they're desperate. This is their last stand, and I'm not going to let them use her like so many people have before. Like I have. So you can get out of my way or get in the vehicle, Ivy. Either way, I'm taking the fight to the people who started this. Maybe then Charlie will finally feel she's earned her freedom, and she can stop running."

"All right." Red hair escaped the tight bun at the back of Ivy's head, something Granger had never seen before in all the years he'd operated at Socorro. The former FBI agent had tried so hard to keep her hands on the reins, but something had happened. She was slipping. "But there's something you need to know before you charge straight at the cartel and start a war."

Ivy handed off her phone. "The coded notes on the blueprints. We weren't able to identify the owner of the handwriting, but Scarlett was able to decipher the notes a few minutes ago."

"How did she find the key so fast?" He read through the translated sentences. He took in times, dates and directions that didn't make any sense.

"It was easy after I explained there was a killer who'd used this code before he disappeared off our radar within *Sangre por Sangre*," Ivy said. "She took a chance on thinking of it like a calling card."

"He used the same key for both codes?" he asked.

"No. This code has been altered. There are only a few

characters left from the original code. It's very sophisticated. Something that would've taken years to create." Ivy took a step into him. "But it did require a three-letter key. Just like the first. Scarlett believed it could be a set of initials."

The notes seemed to indicate a schedule of some kind. But for what? Or who? Henry Acker's name came to mind, but there was no way the general of Acker's Army would be able to waltz into the state capitol building with his face plastered all over federal databases. "Whose?"

"It was Charlie's, Granger," Ivy said.

Granger didn't understand. He pried his attention from the phone. "CGA. Charlie Grace Acker. Why would he use her initials to decrypt notes meant for Henry Acker? As a threat? To keep Acker from forgetting what was on the line?"

"We don't believe he did." The hardness in her voice

Acid surged up his throat as the pieces of Ivy's theory stitched together in the silence between them. "Tell me you're not saying what I think you're saying."

"There's a reason you couldn't find her for those ten years, Granger. Think about it." Ivy's gaze refused to let him go. "You approached Charlie in an effort to gather inside intelligence on Acker's Army. You recruited her to undermine and dismantle her father's organization with the promise to get her and her sisters out from under his control. But Sage and Erin are dead, and she blames him for their deaths. She's hurting. She's angry, and there's no way she can destroy him on her own. What better way to get back at him than by fighting fire with fire?"

"This is insane." Granger maneuvered around Ivy and

headed for his vehicle. "Charlie isn't working with *Sangre por Sangre*. They tried to abduct her. They nearly killed her."

"Unless it was a failed extraction. She survived, Granger. Against all odds. How do you explain that?" Ivy latched onto his arm to get him to stop, and he turned on her.

"Sheer will." He tossed his bag into the back seat and let Zeus climb inside. "She was raised to fight, Ivy. It's all she knows."

"You're right. Fighting is all she knows, except now she has no one to fight. So what do you think is going to happen next?" Ivy asked. "She refused medical care and ran, Granger. Why?"

He didn't have an answer for that.

"You have to move past your feelings and see the truth." Socorro's founder was waiting for him to see reason, but he couldn't. Not when it came to Charlie. "That code we decrypted tells me Charlie Acker is the one calling the shots. And whatever she's planning, she knows we're coming."

Chapter Thirteen

This was the only way to end the bloodshed.

Charlie had no idea if she was in the right place, but *Sangre por Sangre*'s dilapidated headquarters had made headlines over the past two years. There had to be something here that would help make sense of this mess.

She angled the SUV Ivy Bardot had let her take alongside what remained of a parking garage. Boulders of cement and rebar blocked any kind of entrance, but Charlie had snuck into her fair share of construction sites over the years. She knew what to avoid, how to spot a building's vulnerabilities and the general design of structures like this. Her head pounded as she stepped free of the vehicle.

Cool night air mingled with the sweat in her hair. She'd chugged three bottles of water and a couple of ibuprofen from the back cargo area to counter dehydration, but there was no guarantee her self-medicating would do any good. But tucking herself away in Socorro's fortress only delayed the inevitable, and she was tired of hiding. Of pretending she'd made the right choice by running ten years ago. Charlie took that first step toward the building, one of the flashlights she'd found in

the back in one hand. She couldn't ignore the sick feeling in her gut that all of this—Erin's death, her father's
suicide, the cartel's plan for her—wasn't as it seemed.

She needed the truth.

Hesitation wormed through her veins as she approached a hole where the cement hadn't closed off a
section of the underground parking garage. The flashlight beam skimmed over hard cracked earth, not re-
vealing much other than snake holes and ant mounds.
No signs anyone else was here. Or that she was walking
into an ambush. She'd watched the site from the broken
chain-link fence surrounding the property. If the cartel
was still working out of this location, they'd somehow
masked their vehicles, their footprints and their perimeter security.

"It's now or never." Charlie angled the flashlight toward the largest break in the debris. Her body ached as
she climbed through the mouth and into the belly of the
expansive building. Darkness spread out in front of her
as the structure seemed to groan. Dust fell from the ceiling and slipped beneath the scrubs she was still wearing. This was a bad idea, but it was her only option. To
get the truth about Erin. To protect Granger.

Drops of water pattered somewhere inside the collapsed section of garage and echoed off the walls, and
her skin suddenly seemed too tight for her body. A vehicle had crumpled beneath the weight of the ceiling
coming down off to her left, and Charlie couldn't help
but think one wrong move would deliver her the same
fate. The sharp odor of fire and mold collected at the

back of her throat. Parking garages didn't usually stand alone. There had to be an entrance in the main building.

Debris caught on the toe of her boot. She lost her balance for a moment and cut the flashlight across the room. There. A corridor of some kind held its own against the weight of the collapsing structure. Charlie headed straight for it. "Here goes nothing."

Water seeped from the ceiling. Flooding must've occurred upstairs. That explained the cloying scent of mold. Shards of cement flaked off as she ran her fingers against the wall. She followed the hallway to a T, swinging the flashlight from left to right. If the cartel was here, they could come and get her. Finish this. "Hello?"

Her voice seemed to echo on forever, and she suddenly found herself colder than a moment before. There was no way for her to search this entire building alone. Not without getting lost or injured in the process. Her vision swam, and she realized she'd been holding her breath for the past few seconds. She'd made her choice. She'd left Granger and the rest of the Socorro team behind in a twisted attempt to protect them, but the truth was she couldn't even protect herself.

Not really. She'd expended massive amounts of energy trying to hide from the world, isolating herself, moving from one location to the next in an attempt to grant herself one more day of freedom. But it hadn't done a damn bit of good. Because now she was alone. She'd burned the bridges that had sustained her through the past ten years, and no one was coming to fight for her.

Not even the one man she'd trusted to do the job.

Granger had slid back into her life as effortlessly as he had the first time. With promises of protection and concern and respect. He'd been intense—more so than her father—in all the right ways, and had given her something she'd never been granted before: choice. He saw the things she'd tried hiding from her family and the people she'd been raised around, even those she'd tried to hide from herself. Was that what had pressed him to approach her all those years ago and offer her an escape? Had he seen that somewhere deep down she'd never believed in her father's war, that she just wanted to experience the world outside of Vaughn for herself? Somehow, he'd come to know her better than anyone, and Charlie realized, standing in the basement of a crumbling building, surrounded by the putrid stench of death and destruction, she'd never really wanted to be alone after all. She'd just been waiting for him.

Because she was still in love with Granger. Recklessly, ridiculously and resolutely in love with the counterterrorism agent who'd gifted her more than an escape plan ten years ago. He'd given her strength and purpose and trust. Something far more valuable than the inside intel she'd handed over as his confidential informant.

And she'd thrown all of it away out of fear.

Just as she was doing now.

Granger prided himself on never making the same mistake twice. Why was it she couldn't learn from hers?

Charlie directed her attention to the left and followed the corridor as far as it would take her. The power was off, casting her into darkness aside from her flashlight, and it felt as though the walls were slowly closing in.

Which was impossible. Her mind was playing tricks on her. Making her feel as though she were being watched. Like the floor was moving.

There was nothing here, and if there was, she wasn't sure she wanted to stick around to find it. She backed out the way she'd come.

She'd made a mistake coming here. She saw that now. Charlie picked up the pace, trying to remember the turns she'd taken. There were so many, just as there had been in the Socorro headquarters. The hallways weren't meant to make the building easier to navigate. They'd been designed to keep people in, and she felt as though she'd stepped into a prison of her own free will.

Panic clawed at the edges of her mind. Her bones ached, the muscles in her legs had tightened to the point they were pulling on the tendons in the backs of her heels. She couldn't see save for a few feet in front of her, and Charlie could've sworn the shadows up ahead had moved.

She was delirious. Most likely from dehydration and a head injury and the emotions that came from watching her father take his own life right in front of her. It'd all caught up with her, despite her determination to keep running. To never feel as though she couldn't win.

"Let me out of here!" Her own voice echoed back to her as she turned another corner. They all looked the same. Had she come this way? Why the hell hadn't she brought crumbs to mark the way out? Charlie misidentified a corner up ahead. Her shoulder slammed right into it, jarring her back into the moment. Cement crumbled in her hand as she pushed away from the wall. "I want out."

The building moaned as though it'd heard her pleas and mocked them back to her.

She wanted nothing more in that moment than the assurance of her partner and his obese dog. For Granger to tell her they were going to get out of this together. There hadn't been a single moment in the past three days she'd felt as empty and lonely as she did now. She'd always had her sisters or her father or the entire town of Vaughn on her side, even the counterterrorism agent who'd used her for nothing but information. But now? Now she truly had lost everything and everyone she'd convinced herself she could live without. And found she didn't want to. She didn't want to be alone anymore. She didn't want her freedom if it meant isolation. She wanted Granger and Zeus and even Ivy Bardot to have her back. She wanted to be the one the families of her victims could look at and forgive. She wanted a life. "Can anyone hear me? Hello?"

"I hear you," a voice said from the darkness.

Charlie recognized that voice. Though she'd hoped she'd never have to hear it again. She raised the flashlight, but there was no one there. It'd been so clear. So close. Swinging the beam to her left, she followed the corridor. Had her brain played another trick on her? Had she really become so desperate, it'd supplied something for her to focus on? No. It'd been real. "You know why I'm here. I want this to stop."

Her hand shook as she glanced back over her shoulder. The atmosphere had shifted. No longer cold and dark and damp, sweat built under her arms and at the back of her neck.

"That's not for you to decide, Charlie." The words filtered in from the right, but they couldn't have. Nothing but a wall faced her. He was playing games with her. "We're all just following orders here, even you."

"I don't give a damn about your orders." Charlie stopped dead as the corridor opened into a wide alcove. The floor was bare, but her flashlight beam picked up stains of brown spreading out from epicenters. Five, maybe six, in total. Blood. "So you can stop playing your mind games and tell me what the hell the cartel wants me for."

A whisper of an exhale brushed against the back of her neck. "But we were just beginning to have some fun."

Charlie turned, flashlight raised to defend herself.

Pain shot across her face, and the world went black.

GRANGER FLOORED THE ACCELERATOR.

The GPS in Charlie's SUV hadn't moved in the past thirty minutes. She'd headed straight for the abandoned *Sangre por Sangre* headquarters, feeding into the doubts Ivy wanted him to have. But Granger knew her. He knew her better than anyone on his team. "Give me an update."

The sound of Zeus's collar registered from the back seat as though the K9 was waiting for an answer too.

"The GPS hasn't budged." Ivy pressed another bullet into the magazine in her lap. Uneven landscape threatened to tip the ammunition and her weapon to the floor, but she'd done this thousands of times in a thousand different scenarios. She slammed the magazine into the base of her weapon and holstered it alongside her rib cage. "It doesn't mean she's still there, but we'll cross that bridge when we get to—wait. The signal just cut out."

"The cartel must've figured out the SUV is one of ours." Granger had never known Ivy to join any of her operatives in the field, but with the final stage of eliminating *Sangre por Sangre*, the agent had apparently taken it upon herself to see the job through. "She'll be there. And I'll prove she's not the one behind this."

"You're letting your emotions for Charlie get in the way of your assignment, Granger." Ivy kept her attention out the windshield, completely devoid of personality when faced with whatever waited for them at the end of this field trip. "You need to be prepared for the worst-case scenario."

"You're right. I *am* emotional, especially when it comes to her." Granger did what he did best: keeping his voice even while every cell in his body threatened to break apart. "It was my emotions that led me to take a chance on Henry Acker's daughter and turn her into a confidential informant. Without Charlie, Homeland Security never would've gotten the intel about the Alamo pipeline attack and dozens more people might've been injured or killed in the process. It was also my emotions for her that kept me from turning into someone I didn't recognize after I lost my position with the government. She's the one I had on my mind when I heard about a private military contractor looking for operatives, and the one I thought about when I found Scarlett at the wrong end of a knife on that base four years ago. I let Charlie down when she needed me the most, and I promised I would never fail anyone else again. So yeah, I'm letting my emotions for her get in the way of my job. Because she's the reason I fight for people in the first place."

Ivy didn't respond to that and turned her gaze out the passenger side window.

"I know you believe our emotions shouldn't have priority when we're in the field, Ivy, and that policy might've worked for you to some extent when you were with the FBI," he said. "But if we're going to dismantle *Sangre por Sangre* for good, we can't be like them. We have to keep the parts of us that make us human, that make us better."

They drove the rest of the miles in silence.

Granger rolled up to the barbed chain-link fence standing as a warning to those who entered and surveyed the property. *Sangre por Sangre*'s headquarters had been built at the bottom of a manmade crater, a protective layer meant to mask the structure from satellite imagery and keep the cartel off law enforcement's visual radar. He could barely make out the curve of the roof from this distance, but something in his gut told him Charlie was still inside.

She was the key to this whole puzzle, and no matter what Ivy or the rest of his team believed, or how determined Charlie had been to undermine her father's army, she'd never put anyone's life at risk to achieve that goal. The pain of her past mistakes wouldn't let her, and Granger loved her for that. Loved every fiber of her stubborn, perfectionist, passionate being. He was pretty sure he'd never stopped loving her, but these past three days had driven that reality to a point he couldn't shove it down anymore.

Because when it came right down to it, she would sacrifice herself to save someone else. How many operatives on his team would do that for the strangers they tried to protect? Charlie fought for what she believed in, but more importantly, she was afraid of being as corrupt as Henry Acker, and there wasn't a single cell in his body that could believe her responsible for this mess. Whatever was going on, she was just as much a victim as the innocent lives taken the night of the Alamo pipeline attack.

He loved Charlie, and he would do whatever it took to give her the future she deserved. One with him and a fat bull terrier at her side. If she would have him.

Granger let the SUV crawl forward, every instinct he owned on high alert. The south side of the building came into the windshield's frame, and his gut clenched. "This place is on its last legs. If Charlie's in there, she doesn't have long before the whole structure comes down on top of her."

"Then we better get moving." Ivy hit the dirt, using her door panel as cover until they cleared the path leading down into the manmade dust bowl.

Unholstering his weapon, Granger followed her lead as they skidded down the incline. Large chunks of debris and metal scattered across the eighth of mile between the edge of the crater and the building itself. A minefield perfect for an ambush. Except the closer they got to the building, the chances of a surprise attack decreased. "Cash sure made a mess of this place."

And Granger couldn't fault his teammate for that. Not anymore. Socorro's forward scout had literally torn apart an entire building to get to the woman he loved. And Granger would bring the rest of this place down if that was the way to get Charlie back.

They worked their way to what looked to be the remains of an underground parking garage. It was a miracle the structure hadn't collapsed in on itself in this condition, but he would take every second they had left. He and Ivy moved as one, her taking up the rear in case they were attacked from behind. He broke through the perimeter of the garage, dodging massive sections of cement twice his height, and scanned what he could see of the interior. "Clear."

Ivy carved a path over broken asphalt, debris and puddles of water. "There's an entrance on the back wall." She didn't wait for him to acknowledge, cutting across the remains of the garage, and took position at one side of the door. She waited for him, then nodded.

Granger raised his weapon at an angle. The battle-ready tension he'd relied on as he and Charlie had crossed the border into Vaughn snapped into place. Working the plan, learning who the players were and getting the upper hand—this was what he'd been trained for. What he was good at, and up until three days ago, he'd done his job on autopilot. Now he had a goal: to find the woman who made him want to keep going.

He whistled low to call Zeus to heel as the building seemed to swallow them. Hitting the power button to the flashlight along the barrel of his weapon, Granger lit up the few feet ahead of them. The scent of death and humidity burned down his throat. "Find Charlie, Zeus."

The dog trotted ahead, nose to the ground, his belly

swinging back and forth with every step. There were so many competing smells in Granger's senses, he wasn't sure how the K9 would manage to pick Charlie out from among them, but Granger trusted his partner to make the connection.

A low ruff tightened the muscles down the bull terrier's back.

"He can't pick up her scent." Damn it. He'd known that was a possibility, but the stakes were higher than ever. Granger caught up with Zeus and scratched the dog between his ears. "There's too much interference."

"Then we're on our own." Ivy maneuvered ahead, coming up short of a T in the maze. "Which way?"

One wrong turn and they could lose Charlie forever. Granger wasn't willing to take that risk. "Every time we second-guess ourselves, Charlie is in more danger. We can't wander around in the dark. We need a plan. We need to split up. We'll cover more ground that way."

"And if you're wrong about this whole thing and Charlie is the one pulling the cartel's strings? We still don't know what *Sangre por Sangre* is planning." Ivy searched down the right corridor for signs of a threat. "Who's going to save your ass? Because the way I see things, your K9 would rather eat you than protect you."

"That's ridiculous. He's not a cannibal. He just has no control over what goes in his stomach and shaming him isn't going to speed the process along." Granger was avoiding the question, and they both knew it. He didn't want to acknowledge the possibility Charlie had led them into a trap, but he'd be a fool not to account for his own blind spots. "If you're right, and Charlie is the one behind this, I'll do what I have to. Until then, I'm going to operate on the belief she needs my help."

Ivy lowered her weapon and stretched out one hand. "That's one of the reasons I hired you. See you on the other side, Agent Morais."

"Agent Bardot." He shook her hand, knowing that his superior had been fighting her own internal battle since receiving the cartel's surveillance photos of Charlie. The man she'd known as her partner during her stint with the FBI hadn't resurfaced, despite the crumbling of *Sangre por Sangre*'s organization, and Granger couldn't help but think that meant one of two things. Either the agent had chosen to remain loyal to the people he was investigating, or she'd find him dead.

Ivy nodded before heading down the right corridor, leaving Granger to search the left.

"It's you and me, kid." He took the lead. The building seemed to come alive with a groan as they traveled deeper into its heart. Whatever waited for them at the end, Granger was ready.

His future was with Charlie.

And he'd fight like hell to keep it.

Chapter Fourteen

"I see you got my message." This voice was different than her abductor's. Familiar.

Charlie pried her eyes open, instantly overwhelmed in the center of a portable spotlight. Pressure built in her head to the point she wasn't sure her stomach could take it anymore. Then the spotlight cut out.

She faced off with the darkness, trying to see through the shapes her brain summoned to make sense of her surroundings.

The light burned her retinas a second time. Charlie pressed her head against the cold steel at her back. Her wrists were tied, her ankles bound with rope to individual posts. Zip ties would've been so much easier to break through.

The spotlight went dark again.

"What message? I don't know you." The assault to her senses was keeping her from focusing fully. Not to mention the severe dryness in her mouth and the migraine thudding hard at the back of her head. Her abductor. He'd been here. Watching her in the dark. He must've knocked her out. And now she had no sense of time or location. Charlie pulled at the rope, sawing through the first layer of skin at her wrist and aggravating the healing rash she'd sustained during her abduction. Her entire body felt as though it were on fire.

Movement cut across the spotlight as it flicked back on, and a smaller feminine frame was outlined in its glow. "Oh, Charlie. Of course you do. One could argue you know everything about me. Just as I know everything about you. My favorite foods, my favorite book I wanted to read every night before bed. How I hated the taste of homemade toothpaste, and my fear of being excluded from all the reindeer games my big sisters never let me be part of growing up."

Her brain struggled to connect the pieces. "I don't… I don't understand. Who…"

No. It wasn't possible. Charlie pressed her head back into the scaffolding holding her hostage. "You… You died."

The spotlight darkened, and everything inside Charlie wanted to turn it back on to confirm her worst fears.

Light blazed across the space.

And the woman was right there. Standing in front of her with nothing more than three feet between them. Back from the dead. "It felt like that the entire time I was waiting for you to keep your promise. It felt like dying. Over and over, a thousand times."

"Erin." Her sister's name left her mouth as nothing more than a whisper as she battled with logic and exhaustion and confusion. "What have you done?"

"I took control of my life, Charlie. Isn't that what you wanted me to do? Why you ran and left me behind?" Her younger sister sidestepped to Charlie's left, the spotlight highlighting the ten-year difference between the girl she'd known and the woman she'd become. Erin's hair was shorter, cut for convenience rather than inspired by the magazines she'd hidden under her mattress away from their father. Her face seemed thinner. Features Charlie had associated with the fifteen-year-old she'd loved no longer existed. Instead, there was something almost foreign about her. Detached. "There wasn't a single day of the past ten years that I didn't think about you. Not one moment that I didn't wonder if you thought about me."

"Of course I did. Everything I did, every choice I made, was to help you escape Vaughn." Charlie forced herself to stare into the spotlight in order to adapt her vision faster. Another glow pulled at her attention, near where Erin stood. "To finally get you out. But when I heard you'd died… I thought I was too late."

The spotlight went dark.

Leaving the familiar outline of her sister's shape.

And the glow of a barrel fire.

Metallic scraping got her attention and raised goose bumps along Charlie's arms.

"There's that promise again. The same one you told me the night we set the charges on the Alamo pipeline. You were going to find a way out of Acker's Army. I lost count of how many times I went to bed with that hope." Erin's voice had changed. No longer familiar and soothing, but dark. "But instead, you ran away, and you left me and Sage there to die. I managed to escape before police got to the scene. Barely. I waited, you know. For you to come back. For you to keep your promise. But you never came."

The spotlight found a new life.

Exposing the steel rod in Erin's hand. The tip glowed orange, flickering with heat—like a brand—as her sister neared. Erin angled the rod closer to Charlie, letting her feel the scalding heat against her face. Her sister's features took second priority as Charlie focused on the threat of feeling that rod on her skin.

"Erin, you don't have to do this. Please. Dad is dead. You can leave." Her voice shook. Charlie pulled against the ropes as the final conversation between her and her father filtered across her mind in a desperate attempt to come up with something—anything—to neutralize her sister's hatred.

"I already have, Charlie. Don't you understand?" Erin waved the steel poker back and forth, illuminating her own face in the process. A dreamlike daze seemed to relax her sister's expression. "Once I realized you weren't going to keep your promise, I devised my own plan to escape Daddy's control."

Understanding hit. "*Sangre por Sangre.* But how?"

"You remember those construction sites our father used to send us to for explosives?" Erin said. "Every single one of them was owned by the cartel through a number of shell corporations. Upper management may have discovered who was responsible a few months ago after Daddy accidentally let the information slip. The cartel may have then sent one of their lieutenants to take care of the problem. And I may have convinced him we could work together. I would help them salvage what remained of their organization, and, in exchange for that help, they would destroy Acker's Army."

"He knew, didn't he? Dad knew." Why hadn't she seen it before? Why hadn't she put the pieces together before now? "That's why he wouldn't tell me about the deal he made with *Sangre por Sangre*. He was willing to provide manpower and weapons because of you. In his mind, everything he's done has been for our benefit. Yours, Sage's and mine. And giving you up wasn't an option."

Erin stared at the glowing tip of the steel rod. "A mistake on his part. I always thought our father was a hard man who demanded perfection at every turn, but in reality, he was very easily manipulated if you managed to hit the right buttons. And now he's dead."

"That means you're free, Erin. You can live your life without him hanging over your head." Charlie tried to wiggle free from the ropes around her wrists, but her sister had known exactly what she was capable of. The scaffolding she'd been bound to shook, and for the first time since she'd regained consciousness, she realized she and Erin weren't alone. A man stood behind the spotlight. Most likely the one who'd knocked her unconscious in the first place. She lowered her voice to a whisper. "Whatever it is the cartel has planned, whatever they're making you do, you don't have to be a part of it. We can leave. We can start over. Together. You just have to loosen the ropes. I can take care of everything else."

The spotlight died, casting her back into darkness and stealing the hope that'd held her upright.

A laugh Charlie didn't recognize echoed off the walls.

"You still don't understand, do you?" Erin's voice seemed distant now. Alien. Sparks shot up from the floor as her sister dragged the end of the poker along the cracked cement. "*Sangre por Sangre* isn't forcing me to do anything against my will, Charlie. That day the cartel sent a lieutenant to kill our father, I proposed a different plan. To use him and his army to our own advantage. Much the same way that Homeland Security agent approached you."

"What?" Charlie asked.

"You didn't think I knew about him, but it was so clear to anyone who bothered to notice. I noticed," Erin said. "The late-night disappearances from your room. The way you'd smile throughout the day when you didn't think anyone was looking. You changed. You lost your touch during sparring. Like you were distracted. You were more compliant to our father's commands, and I knew something had changed."

The spotlight lit up again, burning Charlie's retinas.

Erin was holding the steel rod back over the edge of the barrel fire, twisting it this way and that, as though she had all the time in the world. "So I followed you. I waited as you slipped out of your bedroom window and met him in the trees. I didn't recognize him at first, but it wasn't long before I realized you'd been selling us out. All of us."

"For you, Erin. I only agreed to give up information on Acker's Army and our father in exchange for the three of us to get free." Didn't she understand that? She'd put her own life on the line for her sisters. Only she'd been too late to save Sage. But she could still help Erin.

"You can tell yourself that all you want, dear sister, but I know the truth." Erin brought the rod back up in front of her. "We were a team, Charlie. You, me and Sage. It was supposed to be the three of us against our father. We were supposed to be together forever, but I saw how you looked at that agent, how much you wanted to please him, and it seems like nothing has changed. You're terrified that he'll be disappointed in you, that he won't have any use for you. You're as weak as he was, you know? The man who raised us. All I have to do is push the right buttons. Fortunately for you, I have a way to fix that."

"What do you mean?" Charlie lost her focus on escape as Erin came back, the steel poker between them. The heat bled through her scrub top. "Fix what?"

"I have a use for you. I can give you purpose again. I can make the past ten years disappear as though they never happened. I have the explosives, thanks to my friends here. All I need from you is your skills in directing the blast," her sister said.

"The blueprints I found in Dad's office." Charlie rushed to make sense of the cartel's motives. "You wanted him and Acker's Army to attack the state capitol. Why?"

"There's something we need." Erin's voice had taken on a wispy quality again. Lighter than it should be, considering the circumstances. "Evidence that was taken from us by the DEA. We know it's being stored in one of their facilities. We just don't know which one, and I'm kind of in a hurry."

"You mean drugs." She couldn't believe this. Her little sister—the perfect innocent girl she'd helped raise—

had sided with a brutal, unforgiving drug cartel. "That's what all of this is about?"

"I gave my word, Charlie. I promised the cartel I would do whatever it took to help them put their organization back together, in exchange for helping me dismantle Daddy's life's work." Erin pulled at the collar of her shirt, exposing angry and twisted scaring along her collarbone. "But first, I need to know you're one of us. That you won't betray me again."

"Erin, please." Survival kicked in. Charlie wrenched her wrists and ankles, but there was no give in the rope.

"Don't worry, Charlie. The pain only lasts a minute." Erin lowered the steel rod against Charlie's shoulder.

The heat burned through her scrub top and past layers of skin. Every muscle in her body fought against the scalding pain of hot steel, but there was no relief. Her scream ripped up the back of her throat.

Erin pulled the poker back. Satisfied. "Then you and I are going to get to work."

THE SCREAM PIERCED through the heavy rhythm of his breathing.

It tunneled past Granger's focus and pulled him up short.

His gut tightened as pain, agony and hopelessness combined into a hot rage in his veins. "Charlie."

Granger picked up the pace. Zeus hadn't been able to pick up her scent yet, but they were getting close. He could feel it. His heart rate hit out-of-control levels the harder he drove himself, but he had no other option. He wasn't going to lose Charlie. Not again. "Go on, Zeus, go get her!"

The bull terrier vaulted ahead despite the extra thirty pounds on his frame. He disappeared around a corner up ahead, and Granger had to trust the K9 would lead him true. The muscles in his legs protested with every step and aggravated the wound along his rib cage, but there wasn't anything in the world that would stop him from getting to her.

Not when he was so close.

Granger rounded the corner, following Zeus's trail.

A gunshot exploded from down the corridor.

He slowed his momentum and listened. Silence seeped through the walls as he waited for a response. Damn it. He'd rip this place apart if something had happened to his K9. He whistled low enough for Zeus to pick up on, a specific tone only the bull terrier would respond to. Granger approached the corner and rounded it without hesitation

A fist flew at him.

He dodged out of the way and threw a right hook at the attacker who'd been waiting for him. His knuckles screamed at the contact, pain vibrating up his wrist and into his arm. Granger palmed the side of the soldier's head and slammed the bastard into the wall. The man collapsed. "Seems I'm in the right place after all."

Another attacked from behind. He managed to block the strike coming straight at his face, then latched onto the soldier's shoulders and threw the second attacker to the cement.

"I've been looking forward to this moment, Agent

Morais," a voice said. "Please give my regards to Agent Bardot."

Ivy? Strong arms wrapped around Granger's neck from behind and threw off his balance. He stumbled back, at the whim of a third soldier tasked with slowing him down. His shoulders hit the wall a split second before a fist rocketed into his face. Lightning struck behind his eyes as momentum threw him to one side. The taste of blood coated the inside of his mouth as another soldier joined in the fun. "The hell do you want with Ivy?"

"She and I go way back." Recognition flared as memories of the attack in the woods surrounding Vaughn rushed to the front of his mind. The man who'd taken Charlie, the cartel lieutenant. "Didn't she tell you? Perhaps when this is all over, I'll pay her a visit myself. Until then, I've been asked to keep you here. Dead or alive—it doesn't matter to me."

"Good luck with that." He kicked at the attacker to his right and jolted the son of a bitch back and gained a bit of freedom in the process.

Granger launched his elbow into the soldier's rib cage. The bastard doubled over and gave Granger the perfect opportunity. Grabbing for the attacker's boot, he threw everything he had into getting the man off his feet. Only the soldier fisted Granger's clothing and brought them down together. Aches charged through his system as he tried to get his bearings. The bullet graze in his side screamed in response. Not to mention tore at the healing muscles in his shoulder. His vest kept him from taking a full breath and only added to the dizziness trying to get the best of him.

A moan filtered through the overactive race of his pulse. He threw a fist into the soldier's face beside him, knocking a piece off the board. Granger struggled to get to his feet, unsure of his own weight. Just as the next strike forced him back down. Pain erupted from his mouth and nose in a blinding flash of heat and agony, but he wasn't going down. Not until he found Charlie.

Granger cocked his elbow back and targeted the son of a bitch in front of him as exhaustion undermined his control. His fist streaked past the soldier he was aiming for, and Granger couldn't help but follow. Faster than he expected, his attack shoved him into the opposite wall of the corridor.

Hunched down, the third soldier angled his shoulder into Granger's gut and hauled him off his feet. One step. Two. Gravity released its hold on him as his opponent slammed him to the floor.

He barely had a second to make sense of his attacker's next move before a knee slammed into his face. The world threatened to spin as Granger tried to regain control of his body. A boot carved into his rib cage and stole the oxygen from his lungs despite the protection of his Kevlar vest.

Granger summoned the last of his adrenaline reserves and put everything he had into getting off the floor. He dug his fingers into the wall for support. Throwing his shoulder into the nearest attacker, he lunged at the man standing between him and Charlie and pulled the soldier off his feet. The muscles in his legs burned as he hauled the added weight through a thin door on the other side of the corridor. They spilled into the room and hit the ground as one.

His mouth filled with blood. Granger spit it out as the pain in his head tried to warn him he was shutting down. Red stains spewed in every direction, creating miniature Rorschach tests on the floor.

Granger pulled a blade from his ankle holster. He arched his arm and buried the tip of the knife into the soldier's thigh. With a twist, he inflicted as much pain as he could to take the cartel member out of commission. Only the bastard wouldn't go down. Granger fisted both sides of the soldier's collar and threw him into the floor face-first.

The cartel lieutenant he'd left in the hallway had come around. He shot straight for Granger's throat and squeezed, pinning him against the floor. "Do you know how many women I've killed for challenging *Sangre por Sangre*? Your FBI agent Ivy Bardot doesn't even know about all the other bodies I buried. She only found the ones I wanted her to find. Now imagine what I'm going do to Charlie when I'm finished. How long do you think it will take you to find her? You and your team of dogs will have to search the entire state to put her back to-gether."

"No." The visual was too much. Pressure built in his head with every second his brain lacked oxygen, but he hadn't come this far to stop now. He maneuvered one hand around the soldier's wrist, broke the suffocating contact with his throat and twisted until the bones of the man's hand snapped.

A scream echoed off the walls as the cartel member

dropped to his knees, and Granger rocketed his fist into the son of a bitch's temple to put him down. "You'll never touch her again with that hand."

The final rush of adrenaline seemed to drain right out of him then, and he stumbled toward the door and back out into the corridor. His brain had a hard time making sense of direction, but there was something pulling him deeper into the building. He sucked in as much air as his lungs could hold, and still, it wasn't enough. Peeling off his Kevlar vest, Granger discarded it on the floor to get a hold of himself. "I'm coming, Charlie. I'm coming."

His boots kicked up chunks of cement as he used the wall to keep him upright. All he had to do was take that next step. To keep moving forward. "Just hang on."

The corridor emptied him out into alcove lined with scaffolding. Spotlights cast too-bright light around the room. A barrel fire burned at one end with a steel poker discarded nearby, its tip still red from heat. The scream. He caught sight of severed rope hanging from one section of the scaffolding and crossed the room. Pulling it free, he rubbed the fibers between his fingers and scanned the rest of the room. Empty. His chest filled with all the longing and grief and rage he'd felt after her disappearance and honed it into a single word. "Charlie!"

The building moaned in response. Dust fell in streams. Then a single chunk of cement from above. The rock exploded upon impact and sent shards in every direction. The entire structure seemed to be suffering right along with him.

A bark cut through the tremors vibrating through the walls.

That single sound washed the failure from his veins and focused his attention to a doorway across the room. Granger discarded the section of rope, jogging for the exit. "Zeus?"

The door dumped him into an area not mapped on satellite imagery. Weapon raised, he cleared each door he passed along the corridor. The scaffolding. There was a reason *Sangre por Sangre* wouldn't let this building fall apart and die where it stood. They were still building in secret. Under the radar from law enforcement and Socorro. Damn it. How long had he and his team let them restructure without notice? Wood beams braced up the ceiling, preventing the shaft from falling in on itself. The unpaved ground slopped downward, and the only place Granger could think where it led was straight to hell.

An earthquake shook the corridor and knocked Granger into the wall. Despite the cartel's determination to keep this building on its last legs, the whole place was about to come down around them. Dirt slid beneath his shirt and into his hair, pushing him to pick up the pace.

He had to move fast.

Granger followed the shaft deeper into the earth as one of the beams fell out of place. A landslide of dirt cascaded behind him. Within seconds, the way he'd come was sealed. Another bark sounded from the darkness ahead. He couldn't focus on a way out right now. All that mattered was getting to Charlie and Zeus. They were his team—his future—and he would do whatever it took to reach them.

He breached an anterior room off the main shaft. And froze.

"It's so nice to finally meet you, Agent Morais." The woman held Charlie at gunpoint. A hint of familiarity pricked at the back of his mind, and Granger found himself looking at a dead woman. "We have so much to talk about."

Chapter Fifteen

Charlie struggled to pick an emotion to feel.

There were just too many, all vying for her attention. The burn on her collarbone screamed with every move of her fingers interlaced behind her head, but no amount of pain could keep her from taking her gaze off Granger.

He'd come for her.

After everything she'd said—everything she'd done—to protect him, he'd once again risked his life in favor of saving hers. A sob shook through her at the thought but cut short as dirt from the ceiling rained down in handfuls.

"You pull that trigger, and it's the last thing you'll ever do, Erin." Granger was slowly closing the distance between them. There was nowhere for them to go. This place was about to cave in, and the three of them would be buried if they didn't leave now.

"Funny. I was about to tell you one more step and I'll pull the trigger." Erin pulled back on the weapon's slide and loaded a round into the chamber. "My father raised me to be the best, Agent Morais. Do you really think you can cross this room before Charlie dies?"

The barrel of Erin's weapon scratched against her

scalp, and Charlie closed her eyes to clear her head. Instead, her mind forced her to face a black pool of ifs and whys. "Erin, please. You can still walk away from this. I know you're scared. I was too when I first got out from underneath Dad's control, but you can do this. We just have to—"

Erin fired a shot into the ceiling. Dirt hit the ground from above, and a crack spread out from the bullet's entry. "Stop trying to convince me we're a team. You were never any good at it, Charlie, even before you disappeared. No. Here's what's going to happen. Agent Morais and his doggy sidekick are staying here while you and I have some quality sister time. On your feet."

Her sister wrenched her arm up, bringing Charlie to stand. "If you so much as move in our direction, I'll shoot her. If you call your dog, I'll shoot her. There is nothing you can do to save yourselves, Agent Morais. I'm the one—"

Charlie wrenched her elbow back into Erin's stomach. She turned as her sister brought the weapon up. Ramming her shoulder into Erin's belly, Charlie tried to knock the gun from her hand. And failed.

"Charlie!" Granger screamed.

Erin buried the heel of her boot in Charlie's chest. The back of her sister's hand made contact and knocked Charlie off her feet. They'd trained together. They'd learned to fight from the same source. There wasn't anything Charlie could do that wouldn't be met with equal or greater force. And, in truth, she didn't want to. She didn't want to hurt her baby sister. Not when she had so many memories of helping raise her. Guilt for not saving her as she'd promised.

She stared up at Erin from the ground as the betrayal and loss and grief she'd suffered at the news of her sister's death washed over her.

"You can't beat me, Charlie. I'm not the same girl you knew back then." Erin buried her boot into Charlie's gut. "I'm stronger than you'll ever be. I always have been, and there's nothing you can do to stop me or *Sangre por Sangre* now."

Her ribs threatened to break under another assault. Charlie gasped for breath, but her lungs refused to inhale. She curled in on herself to relieve the pain sparking through her. Her cough bounced off the failing walls and ceiling.

"Stop!" Granger took a step forward, holding his bull terrier partner back. "Erin, stop. She's your sister."

Erin took aim. At him. "You did this to her. You corrupted her. You turned her into something weak with promises of protection and love. Does she even know Homeland Security never authorized you to make her a confidential informant? Does she know how you failed her, that if something had happened, she wouldn't have been protected at all?"

Granger didn't seem to have an answer for that.

And Charlie didn't care.

Because she would've still taken the risk. Just for the chance to start her own life, outside of Vaughn, away from her father. To go to a movie in a theater and drink as many strawberry milkshakes as she wanted. To see the world and work diner jobs. To be with someone who loved her. She'd make that choice over and over. Granger had given her that chance. He'd given her everything.

"You'll never be free this way, Erin. Dad's still controlling you. It's just with your own fear." Charlie kicked her heel out with everything she had.

Erin's feet swept out from underneath her. Her sister managed to keep herself upright, but the gun hit the ground. Erin had been right. The little girl Charlie had known all her life was gone. Now there was only an emptiness.

Grabbing for the weapon, Charlie brought it up. Her finger slipped over the trigger. Ready to bring all of this to an end.

Erin crushed her hand against Charlie's forearm, and her aim went wide. Her sister regained control of the gun and reached out, latching onto Charlie's neck. And squeezed.

She circled both hands around Erin's wrists as the life drained out of her, but there was no relief. The burn on her collarbone protested even the smallest movements.

Granger rushed forward.

"Now, I'm starting to lose my patience with you both. So here's what's going to happen next." Erin took aim. And pulled the trigger.

A groan registered from behind Charlie. And it was then she knew Granger had been hit. Every cell in her body honed in on letting go of the feelings attached to her sister. She twisted out of Erin's hold and gasped for air.

Just as nearly a hundred pounds of K9 weight vaulted over her.

Zeus collided with Erin and brought her down. The

bull terrier did what he did best while playing his favorite game and sat on her sister's chest with his full weight. The gun knocked free of Erin's hand and skittered out of reach.

The ceiling shook above them, bringing Charlie's attention up. "Granger, we've got to get out of here." She didn't hear a response, cutting her gaze to the unmoving man on the ground. Her heart shot into her throat. "Granger!"

Dragging herself upright, she let gravity lead her way to him and collapsed at his side. Blood spread over the same shoulder he'd taken a bullet in two months ago. She pressed her hand to the wound, watching as a pool of blood seeped out the back. It was a through and through. Easily treated as long as they got out of this mess.

"Why do people keep aiming for this shoulder?" His attempt to lighten the mood worked better than she wanted it to. "Hasn't it been through enough?"

The shaft walls started to crumble around them. Zeus sneezed from the added dust in the air.

"Come on. You need to stand. We've got to go." Taking his weight, Charlie angled her shoulder beneath his arm. His face had been battered. He seemed to be covered in blood no matter where she looked, but he was alive. They were both alive. For the time being. "Zeus, let's go."

The K9 obeyed, leaving Erin gasping for breath.

Her sister clawed for the weapon just out of reach. "I'm not finished, Charlie. You owe me. You owe me ten years of waiting!"

"No, Erin. I don't. Because you're still stuck in the

past, and I was brave enough to go after my future."
Charlie turned to face her as the ceiling collapsed directly onto her sister. Dust billowed out from the hole in the ceiling and spread faster than she expected.

"Run!" Granger clutched onto her hand and pulled her through the opening. He kept her at his side as the walls seemed to disintegrate right in front of her eyes.

Her legs protested with each step, but they couldn't slow down. They couldn't stop. Zeus raced ahead of them like that reindeer she'd read about as a kid helping Santa through the fog on Christmas Eve.

Except part of the shaft had collapsed in front of them.

She could see the other side. Light permeated from the other end of the tunnel, but there was no way for them to get to it. Wood beams and an oversized mound of dirt had cut them off. "Start digging!"

Zeus took the order with enthusiasm and started using both paws to dig. Charlie bit back the pain of her branded shoulder and the relentless pain in her skull as she grabbed for handfuls of dirt from the top of the mound.

But the ceiling was still caving in. With every scoop they got out of the way, the earth seemed to want to fill the void, and they had to start again. Dirt kicked up into the air and drove down into her lungs. If tens of thousands of tons of earth didn't crush them, they would die of suffocation. A rumble shifted the ground underneath her feet, and Charlie looked back to see the shaft collapsing in on itself.

"Granger." His name left her mouth as nothing more than a whisper. They'd run out of time. No matter how many minutes they'd made up for these past three days, it was never going to be enough.

"Don't give up." Granger secured her in his arms as the wave of dirt and debris drew near. "I love you. I'm always going to love you."

"I've loved you ever since that night you offered me a strawberry milkshake. You changed my life for the better, and I'll never be able to thank you for that," she said.

"Granger!" A voice cut through the low groan of the building coming down on top of them. A single hand drove through the mound of loose dirt. "Grab hold of the rope!"

Someone had offered them a lifeline.

"Go!" Granger maneuvered Charlie up the side of the mound, and she wrapped the rope around her wrist. "Pull!"

Charlie took a deep breath as though she were about to dive for the Olympics. Her arm stretched through to the other side as thousands of pounds of dirt threatened to crush her, but there was another force on the other end. One that wanted her to live.

She broke through the wall of debris to find Ivy Bardot on the other end. Untwisting the rope from around her wrist, she shoved it at Socorro's founder. "We need to get them out of there!"

"Granger, rope!" Ivy speared the ratty fibers back through the wall of dirt as the ground shook beneath their feet.

"Pull!" Granger's voice boomed through the space on the other side, and Charlie and Ivy worked together to get Zeus through the limited opening.

The bull terrier shook layers of dust from his coat and sneezed three times before circling around Charlie's feet. Untying the knot on his collar, she drove the end of the rope back through the mound. "Granger!"

Only there was no response.

The rope remained slack, and the seconds slipped through her fingers as easily as the grains of sand through an hourglass. "Granger."

She drove both hands into the mound, searching for a sign he'd survived the collapse.

And pulled a single hand free.

Two days later...

DYING IN A shaft collapse hadn't hurt so bad.

Granger tried to sit up in the recovery bed, but the mattress and pillows were too damn soft. He kept sinking down into the middle as if he'd been ordered to recover in the middle of a marshmallow.

The lights were too dim. His body kept trying to go to sleep on him, but he wanted to stay awake for updates from the team.

Two bodies had been recovered in the bowels of *Sangre por Sangre*'s headquarters. The third soldier who'd attacked him—the one intent on making his relationship with Ivy clear—hadn't been found. Seemed the son of a bitch was good at dodging death. Though Socorro's fearless leader didn't seem bothered by Charlie's description of her abductor, Granger was fairly certain the man Ivy and her partner suspected of killing those women all those years ago and the one Granger had knocked

unconscious were one and the same. Which meant Socorro's undercover source within the cartel couldn't surface. At least not yet.

Scarlett had decrypted all of the notes written in the
margins from the blueprints taken from Henry Acker's
office, including the cartel's final goal: retrieving the
massive amount of fentanyl pills confiscated from *Sangre por Sangre* less than a month ago. Turned out, the
government had only been on the lookout for the pills
because of a sample collected by Scarlett in a ware-
house raid to save a DEA agent's son. Six million dollars' worth. Enough to put *Sangre por Sangre* back on
top of the drug hierarchy, so long as they were able to
liquidate their inventory.

A knock registered from the door, and Charlie—in
all her gauzed and bandaged glory—leaned against the
doorframe. "Up for some company?"

"As long as it's you." Granger relaxed back against the
pillow, taking in everything he could about her.

"This is killing you, isn't it? Having to lay here and
recover like a good operative," she said.

She wasn't wrong. "Doc had one of my teammates
drag me back when I tried to leave. Said she'd sedate
me the next time."

"Patience has never been your strong suit." She
brushed a section of his hair off his forehead, exposing
the gauze beneath her shirt collar. "Mine either. I think
that's why we get along so well."

Her smile took his attention off the ache in his shoulder, but more, it gifted him a knot of hope. That they

could move on from this. Together. "How are things in Vaughn?"

"Chaotic, but Acker's Army has officially disman-tled. Once I informed the residents my father was dead and why, there didn't seem to be any interest for anyone else to step forward." She skimmed her fingers down his arm, raising goose bumps in her path. "His legacy is dead, and the families of the people he hurt will be able to move on now. Just like we always dreamed of."

"I'm sorry about your father, Charlie. I know a part of you still loved him," he said.

"Yeah. Deep down, I believed him when he told me everything he did, everything he put us through, was meant to make us stronger, so we didn't have to suf-fer like he did. That's what fathers are supposed to do, right?" Her expression smoothed over. She was retreat-ing again, holding herself back from having to feel the grief that came with losing a parent. In time, Granger trusted she would learn to deal with it, but for now, he'd let her grieve how she felt she needed to. "But at the same time, look at what happened to Sage. What happened to Erin." She straightened. "Were they able to recover my sister's body?"

"Yeah. Turns out that tunnel wasn't the only one. Once the engineers were able to map out one that ran parallel, they managed to get the excavators in and clear out the collapse." He'd been lucky. Just a few more seconds and Granger would've suffocated right along with Charlie's sister. Lost forever. But she'd pulled him out. "She's with the medical examiner in Albuquerque."

"Good. I know what she did was terrible and hurt a

lot of people, but she didn't deserve to stay down there," she said. "I guess I'm the one who gets to choose where she goes."

"You have a place in mind?" he asked.

"She tried to get out of Vaughn her entire life. I don't think it would be fair to take her back."

"What about your safe house?" He twisted his torso toward the nightstand on the other side of the bed. The bullet graze along his rib cage didn't like the movement one bit, but this was important. "Maybe this could be buried with her."

He handed her Erin's journal, the one she'd taken from her sister's room the first night she'd come back to New Mexico.

"We used to write each other notes in a journal like this. In a special code only the two of us knew. Just in case Dad started snooping." She flipped through the pages, landing on the last entry. "She kept it up. Even after I left, she was writing me notes."

"Come here." Granger brought her head to his chest, below his newest bullet wound. "She was going to kill you, Charlie. I couldn't let her take you from me again."

A line of tears glistened in her eyes. "I know. I just wish she hadn't decided to let her anger and fear make her choices. Maybe then she'd still be alive."

"Maybe," he said.

The click of nails echoed down the hallway. A thud slammed into the recovery room door. The entire frame threatened to break under whatever had hit it.

"I'm going to take a wild guess that Zeus is here to

see you." Charlie pried herself from the edge of his bed and answered the door.

The bull terrier took the invitation without hesitation and launched himself onto the bed. Granger's legs instantly regretted the added weight as he wrestled with the K9 one-handed. "I missed you too, buddy. I hope Charlie's been taking good care of you these past couple days."

"Well, he really took more care of me than I did of him, isn't that right?" She scratched Zeus between his ears, and the dog seemed to melt.

Great. Granger was never going to be able to get out of this bed between the two of them.

"How's the shoulder?" she asked.

"No shards left behind. Seemed the second bullet pushed the shrapnel from the first out. Dr. Piel called it a shot in a million." Granger settled back in the bed, no longer feeling as though he needed to leave. Instead, he wanted to remember everything about this moment. "I'm feeling better than I have in a long time. Then again, maybe it has something to do with the possibility of seeing you once I get out of this bed."

Her smile chased back the numbness starting in his toes and reinvigorated his nervous system. It was a smile only he saw, a spark that couldn't be contained. And he was lucky enough to witness it now. She leaned over the edge of the bed and pressed her mouth to his. "I didn't realize I had such an influence on your recovery. Maybe I should visit more often."

"I like the sound of that," he said.

"I just have one question for you before I agree to anything." There was a brightness in her eyes he hadn't seen in far too long, and Granger couldn't help but lose himself in it. "Do you like strawberry milkshakes, Agent Morais?"

"I would kill for a strawberry milkshake right now, but I think I'm beginning to like this even more." He fisted her jacket and pulled her in for another kiss. The taste of her spread across his tongue and quieted all of the violent memories he'd held onto these past few weeks. It wasn't the mere physical act of having her here but the connection. To her.

"I think I can come around to your way of thinking." She whispered the words against his mouth. "For a price."

"Whatever it is, I'm willing to pay it." There was no arguing about that. He didn't care what she required of him. He would do whatever it took to keep from losing her again. "As long as it gets me you."

"Tell me you love me," she said.

"I love you, Charlie." He set his uninjured hand against her face, and Zeus instantly took that to mean he needed attention too. The dog army-crawled up Granger's chest and set that wet nose against his chin. "I think I fell in love with you the night I met you in your father's backyard with a rifle pointed at my heart, and I was too much of a coward to say it."

It wasn't sudden. It was three months of trusting her as his confidential informant, ten years of building her up in his mind and four days of fighting with her at his side. No matter the circumstance, she'd been right here with him. "And I want you to know, official paperwork or not, I never would've let anything happen to you while under my supervision. Ever."

"I knew, Granger. I knew Homeland Security wasn't going to consider me an official confidential informant because of my relationship to my father." Charlie pressed her face into his hand, planting a kiss in his palm. "Your superior contacted me. He tried to convince me to sever my contact with you, but I didn't care. I made the choice to trust what you were doing. Because we were a team."

"Then and now." And he wouldn't have it any other way.

"Forever," she said. "So, Agent Morais, how about that milkshake?"

He searched the window facing out into the corridor and clocked the security camera posted outside. "We can have all the milkshakes you want if you get me out of this room without anyone else finding out."

"Good thing I have experience with disappearing." She kissed him again. "You've got a deal."

* * * * *